CUMBRIA LIBRARIES
3 8003 04848
KT-547-611

MEGAN RIX is the winner of the Stockton and Shrewsbury Children's Book Awards, and has been shortlisted for numerous other children's book awards. She lives with her husband by a river in England. When she's not writing, she can be found walking her gorgeous dogs, Bella and Freya, who are often in the river.

Books by Megan Rix

THE BOMBER DOG

ECHO COME HOME

THE GREAT ESCAPE

THE GREAT FIRE DOGS

THE HERO PUP

THE RUNAWAYS

A SOLDIER'S FRIEND

THE VICTORY DOGS

WINSTON AND THE MARMALADE CAT

EMMELINE AND THE PLUCKY PUP

www.meganrix.com

The Paw House

megan rix

PUFFIN

PUFFIN BOOKS

UK | USA | Canada | Ireland | Australia
India | New Zealand | South Africa

Penguin Books is part of the Penguin Random House group of companies
whose addresses can be found at global.penguinrandomhouse.com.

www.penguin.co.uk
www.puffin.co.uk
www.ladybird.co.uk

First published 2018
001

Cover illustration by Angelo Rinaldi

Set in 13/16 pt Baskerville MT
Typeset by Jouve (UK), Milton Keynes
Printed and bound in Great Britain by Clays Ltd, Elcograf S.p.A.

A CIP catalogue record for this book is available from the British Library

ISBN: 978-0-241-36910-4

All correspondence to:
Penguin Books
Penguin Random House Children's
80 Strand, London WC2R ORL

No act of kindness, no matter
how small, is ever wasted . . .

Aesop

Chapter 1

Before I went to stay at the Paw House I really wasn't sure I liked animals. My mum certainly didn't like them because she said they were dirty and left fur all over the carpet and licked their bottoms. My dad didn't like them because they made him sneeze.

None of my friends at school had pets, except for Omar, who had a cat. But it hid behind the sofa or under Omar's bed whenever I went to visit, which was a shame because I was *always* watching funny cat videos on YouTube and was desperate to film one of my own. I even set up a YouTube channel for it so I could be ready when the day came.

'The sad fact is,' I told Omar one day, 'animals just don't *like* me. Maybe I smell wrong!' Mum was always saying there's no need to drown myself in body spray when I go out.

'Yeah,' Omar laughed. 'Or maybe animals know you're nervous of them.'

Whatever it was, I just *wasn't* a natural animal person like some people. When I was a little kid our class got taken to Edinburgh Zoo and one of the chimpanzees came up to the glass and stuck its index finger up its nose right next to me.

'That's disgusting!' I told it, outraged. My mum made me wear mittens for weeks when she'd caught me doing that.

Everyone around me burst out laughing. But it wasn't funny. That chimp should have known better than to pick its nose in public.

'I think he likes you, Hamish,' Miss Gregor said, patting my head.

I stared into the chimpanzee's deep dark angry eyes and I wasn't so sure. Those eyes gave me nightmares for years.

Last year I tried to capture the chimp's expression for an art competition run by Creative Edinburgh for Junior High School students. I decided not to do a painting but made a papier-mâché sculpture instead. I worked really hard on it but I knew I hadn't got the chimp's expressive eyes quite right. In my memory he was angry but in my sculpture his eyes looked sad.

Maybe I should call it 'Longing to Return to the Wild,' I thought as I put the sculpture carefully into a cardboard box to transport it to the Scottish National Gallery of Modern Art.

I want to be an artist when I grow up and I was really pleased, and amazed, when the judges awarded me first prize. I got to have a photograph of me and my forlorn-eyed chimp sculpture in the *Scotsman* newspaper.

That day at the zoo was the most time I'd ever spent with animals before I went to stay at the Paw House. Maybe if we'd lived in the countryside it would have been different, but we live in an apartment along the Royal Mile in Edinburgh – not very animal-friendly! Plus, apart from my room, the whole place is decorated in immaculate cream and white. Mum doesn't like anything to be out of place. It gives her headaches.

'A tidy home shows a tidy mind,' she always says. She'd probably lay down and die rather than live at the Paw House. My mum and dad run their own interior design business and they're really, really good at it. They get to go all over the world telling people how places should look and sometimes I get to go with them and stay in posh hotels too.

But the summer this story starts was different. They were heading off to Japan, one of the places I most wanted to visit in the whole world.

'Sorry, Hamish . . .' Dad said.

'Our schedule is packed tight – we can't have you tagging along and getting in the way,' said Mum.

I resisted pointing out that they didn't exactly rush around trying to entertain me when they *were* at home.

'I won't get in the way,' I promised desperately.

'We'll be out all day meeting clients and you'd be bored silly,' Dad told me.

'I could help . . .'

Dad looked at Mum and then shook his head.

I should have known they wouldn't listen to me. They almost never do. Hamish: their very own invisible son. My name used to get shortened to Mish – until Omar told me it meant 'not' in Arabic.

'As in *mish mumkin* or "not possible"!' he'd laughed.

Now I'm trying to change it to Mishka after the 'Keep Watch' cartoon-eyeball logo streetwear.

Mum and Dad both started speaking at the same time.

'So we've asked my sister, your Aunt Helen . . .' Mum said.

'You wouldn't believe how hard it was to find anyone willing to . . .' Dad added.

Mum gave him one of her looks and he clamped his mouth shut.

'. . . and she said she'd love to have you visit her,' Mum told me.

Aunt Helen was one of those relations I got a Christmas and a birthday card from each year but never actually saw.

'Have I met her?' I asked.

Mum gave a weird fake laugh. 'Of course. When did Hamish last see Helen, Malcolm?'

Dad frowned. 'Cousin Laura's wedding maybe?'

'No, she didn't go to that,' Mum said.

'Your dad's funeral?'

'Yes – she came back to his house at Cullen Bay for that.'

This was hopeless. How was I supposed to remember anyone from my grandad's funeral nearly two years ago? I'd hardly been able to see anything through my tears.

'Well, she was definitely at the christening.'

I looked from my mum to my dad and sighed. I was pretty sure they meant *my* christening.

'What does Aunt Helen even look like?' I asked.

'A lot like your mother,' Dad said. 'Has the same glorious red hair. You'll have no trouble recognizing her at the train station.'

'Station?' It came out as more of a squeak than I'd intended. I didn't know their plan to palm me off was so advanced. I swallowed and lowered my voice. 'What station?'

'Strathcarron.'

I'd heard of it vaguely but couldn't quite place it.

Mum saw my confused face and looked cross. 'Your geography's hopeless!'

'It's in Wester Ross, not far from Lochmarron and Lochcarron,' Dad said. 'Beautiful place.'

'Strathcarron's the nearest station to her sanctuary, which is just outside Lochmarron,' Mum added.

'Sanctuary?' I said, intrigued. Did Aunt Helen run a health farm? Were there going to be massages and Jacuzzis on tap? Maybe this summer wasn't going to be so bad after all. Free treatments for visiting relatives, I hoped. Maybe even a mud wrap! They're supposed to make your skin super soft.

'You'll need to change at Inverness,' Mum said.

'Don't worry, we'll drop you off at Edinburgh Waverley on the way to the airport,' Dad told me.

'When?' I asked.

'Tomorrow.'

'Tomorrow!'

There was barely enough time to shop for a new health-farm-appropriate wardrobe. I grabbed my wallet.

'Where are you going?' Mum called after me as I headed to the front door.

'To buy some new swimming trunks,' I said over my shoulder.

'Oh, you won't need anything new . . .' she started to say, as I pulled the door open. 'Just make sure you take some warm clothes – and that jumper we got you for Christmas. It can get cold in the Highlands!'

Chapter 2

Lots of people think Scotland is quite small, but it isn't. I couldn't help thinking about how huge and wild and beautiful it was as I stared out of the window.

The train headed on upwards through the countryside, taking me further and further away from Edinburgh and everyone I knew. I still couldn't believe my parents had jetted off without me.

Inverness was the first stop for me, three and three-quarter hours after leaving Edinburgh Waverley station.

As soon as I got off the train I spotted a burger stand and bought myself one with a little of the money my parents had given me to tide me over. It had been *hours* since breakfast and I badly needed something to eat. I unwrapped the burger as I stared up at the information board. Where was Strathcarron? I couldn't see it anywhere.

I hurried over to a station worker. 'I'm supposed to be going to Strathcarron,' I said helplessly.

'You need the train for Kyle of Lochalsh,' the station worker told me, pointing across the concourse. 'Leaving from Platform 7. But you'd better be quick; it's about to go!'

'Thanks!' I called over my shoulder as I ran.

Hundreds of travellers seemed to get in my way on purpose, and my bag bumped against more than one of them and I almost fell over a stray suitcase as I raced across the slippery floor. But the train was still waiting on the platform and I stumbled on board, gasping for air. I hadn't thought to buy a drink and now I only had a dry, lukewarm, chewy bit of burger in a bun. It didn't even have ketchup or mustard on it because I hadn't wanted to risk dripping any on my best jeans.

The train pulled away a few seconds later.

It was much smaller than the one from Edinburgh and full of tourists visiting the Highlands. My right leg was squashed against the hairy bare knee of an elderly American man wearing a kilt. I crossed my legs to get away.

'Visiting my ancestral home,' he kept telling anyone who would listen. 'Might even try throwing the hammer at the Highland Games!'

He tried to tell me too but, even though I knew it was rude, I looked out of the window instead of replying. There was lots to see out there, including waterfalls and rippling streams. Staring at them made me feel even more thirsty. I swallowed hard.

Mountains beyond the river. A herd of shaggy brown Highland cattle.

The man in the kilt fell asleep and snored.

'Look!' a small girl cried out excitedly, and she pointed out of the window at a red deer darting away in the distance.

A bird of prey flew across the bright blue sky.

'Golden eagle!' said the American, who had woken up and was now rubbing his eyes.

'Tourist eagle!' a man on the opposite side of the aisle said. 'That's a buzzard.'

Two and a half hours later the train drew into the station at Strathcarron and people bumped into each other as they grabbed their suitcases and bags.

I'd been travelling for more than six hours and left all I knew behind me before nine o'clock this morning. It was now half past three. I looked out of the window at the mountains in the distance.

I wasn't in such a hurry to get off the train as the rest of the passengers. In fact, the nearer we'd got the more I'd found myself wishing the journey could continue. Lulled on and on by the soft rhythmic clackity-clack of the train.

But I couldn't stay on board forever. There were Jacuzzis and mud wraps and facials waiting for me. I pulled on my black leather jacket and picked up my bag. I was the last to leave the train.

On the platform I looked around for someone waiting for me. Someone who looked like Mum.

But Aunt Helen, it turned out, didn't look like my mother at all. For a start Aunt Helen's long red hair looked like it could do with a good brush. Mum's hair never, ever, *ever* looks like that. It wouldn't dare. It's tamed with a brush and tons of hairspray every morning. And she'd have given the torn jeans and baggy top that Aunt Helen was wearing to the charity shop.

'Hamish?' the woman I'd guessed was Aunt Helen said, coming towards me. 'Hello! I'm your Aunt Helen.'

'It's Mishka,' I said.

'Sorry?' Now she looked confused, as if she wasn't sure I was the right boy after all.

'My name's Hamish but I like to be called Mishka, after the urban streetwear designer,' I said quickly.

'Oh, I see!' she said. 'Nice to meet you, Mishka.'

She hadn't made a fuss about my name change at all! I'd been trying to get people to call me Mishka for ages but it's never quite stuck.

I followed Aunt Helen over to her car, which was parked on the side of the road.

'Here we are,' she said, opening the back so I could put my bag in.

I hadn't really thought about what sort of car a health farm owner might drive, but I wouldn't have expected it to be an old jeep. An old jeep that had an odd smell about it and was very tatty and in need of a good wash – both inside and out!

'Sorry about the car,' she said. 'It's just about impossible to keep it clean with the dogs and other animals, leaving mud and fur all over the place.'

'Dogs?' I gulped. Mum and Dad hadn't mentioned dogs. 'How many dogs?'

'There are five at the sanctuary at the moment,' Aunt Helen said, pulling away from the kerb. 'Mackenzie, Blue, Darcy, Violet and Miss Lily. But sometimes I have more.'

More than five dogs! I didn't say it out loud because she might think I was an idiot if I kept repeating everything she said. But I wasn't looking forward to meeting Aunt Helen's five dogs at all.

'They'll love you,' she told me.

'Who will?'

'The dogs, of course! They're all very friendly and such characters. I can't wait for you to meet them.' Aunt Helen gave me a warm smile.

I gave a little shudder at the thought.

'Cold?' Aunt Helen asked me.

I shook my head. 'It must be hard running a health farm and having lots of dogs to look after as well,' I said. The two didn't seem to go together really.

Did health farms offer treatments for dogs and cats too? Were there mud wraps for dogs and fish face-masks for cats?

It could actually be a good business opportunity. I began to wonder about the sorts of treatments the owners would want for their pets. Would the dogs have their own pool?

Aunt Helen looked over at me, which I didn't think was a good idea at all. Hands on the wheel and eyes on the road, please!

'You're right. I suppose it *is* a health farm in a way,' she said slowly, turning her attention back to the road. 'Although they're usually called sanctuaries. It's certainly a lot healthier for the animals that live there than where they were before.'

Now it was my turn to stare at her. What on earth was she talking about?

'Most people call places like mine animal sanctuaries . . .' Aunt Helen said as she spotted my expression.

My mouth fell open. 'So it's not a – I mean, you don't have a – But what about massages?'

'Sometimes I massage the dogs. Blue loves them and lies there with a big doggy smile on his face . . .'

I looked over at Aunt Helen who had a big smile on her face too.

Can dogs really smile? I thought.

'Whenever I massage Mackenzie he puts out a paw to say *more please*,' she continued. 'I expect all the animals at the sanctuary would like massages really, not just the dogs – just the same as people do. They're so relaxing.'

I thought about the swimming trunks I'd brought, despite my parents' insistence I didn't need them. What a waste!

'Jacuzzis?' I asked in desperation.

Aunt Helen shook her head.

My dreams were shrivelling.

'A swimming pool?'

'There's a duck pond. More and more wild ducks are turning up all the time and swimming about on it.'

I was feeling a bit sick, partly due to the narrow winding lanes we were heading down, but mostly due to the deceit of my parents. They must have known Aunt Helen's sanctuary was for animals and not where people go to relax. They should have told me! And considering how much they hated animals, they must have been pretty desperate to get rid of me to send me *here*. I shuddered again.

Aunt Helen was still talking, the smile still on her face. 'I can't wait for you to meet all the different animals. They're such a nice bunch, with huge personalities. I just can't understand why some of their owners didn't want them! I would have *loved* a dog of my own when I was your age, and your mum wanted one too. But your grandma wouldn't allow it.'

'Really?' I couldn't imagine my mum with a dog. I couldn't imagine her with any pets at all.

'I'd never abandon a dog, or any animal. How could anyone?' Aunt Helen went on, and I didn't know if I should answer or not. 'Sometimes I think I like dogs better than people!'

But she couldn't mean it, of course. No one could like dogs more than people.

We drove on in silence for a while, me staring out of the window, wondering how close my parents were to Japan. They had to fly from Edinburgh to Helsinki and then Helsinki to Tokyo.

The next instant a huge black-and-tan dog ran out into the road in front of us. Aunt Helen slammed on her brakes and swerved to avoid hitting it.

The dog stood in the middle of the road, its great long tongue lolling out, staring at us.

'Ah! That's Homer,' Aunt Helen said. 'He comes over to the sanctuary sometimes – mostly looking for something to eat.'

Three boys about my age stood at the edge of the road close to a sign that read 'Welcome to Lochmarron'. I couldn't see their faces clearly because they were wearing hoodies. In their hands they held cans of spray paint and I couldn't help but notice that there was an awful lot of paint on the sign.

I love street art and graffiti. Spray painters can be so skilful and talented. But these three definitely hadn't been trying to create art. There was no thought behind their slashes of paint – the sign was a mess.

'Get out of the way, Homer, you idiot,' the biggest of the boys shouted.

'That's Cyrus,' said Aunt Helen. 'Homer's his dog – poor thing.'

The dog picked up a ball from the centre of the road, but instead of running out of the road again he sat down and started to lick the ball.

A car came up behind us and honked its horn.

Aunt Helen turned off the engine and unclipped her seat belt. 'I'd better see . . .'

'Get over here, stupid,' the other two boys called to the dog.

'That's Donald, who likes to be called Donut, and Jamie, who prefers Jay,' said Aunt Helen with a sigh. 'Good boys really. Apart from when Cyrus comes home for the holidays. Easily led.'

The dog picked up his ball and padded over to them.

Aunt Helen shrugged, reclipped her seat belt and started the engine again.

I looked back as we drove off, just in time to see Cyrus throw his can of paint after the car. He was a useless shot and it missed by miles.

'Sorry about them,' Aunt Helen said. 'They think they own the village and can do what they like.'

'Looks like they can,' I said, still looking behind us.

Cyrus was now pointing his finger at me and shouting. I couldn't hear what he was saying but I could understand his gesture well enough. I was glad I was safely sitting inside the car and not out there.

Aunt Helen drove on.

Chapter 3

Soon Aunt Helen stopped at a wide farm gate. Next to the gate was a black-and-white shaggy-coated dog that looked a lot smaller than the one we'd just met. The dog was lying down as the car approached, but it jumped up and started wagging its tail like crazy as we got nearer.

'It's only got three legs!' I said in surprise. One of the dog's back legs was missing.

'That's Mackenzie,' Aunt Helen told me. 'And believe me, he manages just fine with three. He's the reason I now run the sanctuary. One day I was on my way home, thinking about buying this place and starting a new venture, when out of the corner of my eye I saw him lying at the side of the road. I wasn't even sure he was a dog at first; he could have been a deer or a badger. I could easily have carried on driving . . .'

'Lucky you didn't,' I said.

'I don't know how long he'd been lying there for,' Aunt Helen continued. 'His leg was so badly infected it couldn't be saved. I wrapped him in my car blanket, put him in the car and drove back to my friend Sheena's veterinary practice. Luckily she was working late and could see him straight away, although she wasn't sure if he'd survive either. But thank goodness he did and this place became Mackenzie's home. The first guest.'

'His owners never came forward to claim him then?' I asked.

Aunt Helen pressed her lips together and shook her head. 'No they didn't. Would you mind opening the gate, please, Mishka?' I must have looked a bit worried because she added, 'Mackenzie won't hurt you.'

'Sure,' I said as I got out of the car. I wasn't frightened of the small shaggy-coated dog, not really. I'd just try not to get too close.

But as it happened Mackenzie wasn't the least bit interested in me. As soon as I started to open the gate he raced through it and went running to the jeep. Aunt Helen opened the car door and I could hear her laughing as I pushed the gate fully open.

'Yes, I missed you too!'

When I looked back at the jeep I saw Mackenzie was now sitting in my seat and looking at me through the window.

It was spitting with rain and I was glad of my leather jacket. The ground here was muddy and my cream-coloured retro canvas shoes weren't really designed for it. But at least it felt good to be standing up after such a long time travelling. I breathed in the fresh Highland air and then immediately coughed at the less pleasant, more manure-ish, additions I could smell.

I gave a flourishing bow to Aunt Helen as I waved her car through the gate and although I couldn't hear her laughing I could tell by her face that she was.

When I got back in the car I saw that Mackenzie had one brown eye and one blue, and must have been quite old because there was grey mixed in with his black-and-white fur. He politely hopped into the back where I could hear him panting and feel his hot breath on my neck. It made me squirm.

Aunt Helen drove on down the potholed driveway and we passed a few decrepit outbuildings before stopping outside a house that badly needed a lick of paint. As soon as we got out of the car I could hear the sound of dogs. Lots of dogs, *big dogs*, barking very loudly.

Aunt Helen looked over at my worried face. 'You're not frightened of dogs, are you?'

'Haven't had much experience of them,' I admitted.

'Let's say hello to the other animals we have here first,' she said.

I nodded. Good idea.

Mackenzie jumped out of the jeep and followed us.

'This place was only supposed to be for rescue dogs initially, but you know what it's like,' Aunt Helen said, as the three of us headed towards the outbuildings. I didn't tell her that I had no idea at all what it was like, and she continued. 'It started off with just Mackenzie . . .'

The shaggy-coated dog looked up at her at the sound of his name.

'But then more and more dogs came. It's just about impossible to turn any animal in desperate need away. And once people hear you're willing to take in waifs and strays you soon become inundated with them! Just today I agreed to take on a donkey and foal that need a place to stay. Only, my savings have just about all gone now, and if I don't get at least some of the dogs new homes I won't be able to take in any more –' She suddenly seemed to remember I was there. 'Oh! What am I going on about? You don't want to hear me moaning. Let's get you introduced.'

I was just wondering exactly what other animals Aunt Helen had (and if they'd be friendly) when she pulled open the door to a large barn and a very fat Highland cow with huge horns and a wavy orange coat mooed at us. It sounded just like it was saying *hello* in cow talk, only I didn't say that to Aunt Helen in case she thought I was crazy. Mackenzie sniffed at the cow's nose and the cow sniffed back at him.

Before I could stop myself I blurted out, 'Are they saying hello to each other?'

Aunt Helen didn't seem to think I was crazy at all. 'Oh yes, I think so – don't you?' She smiled.

I'd never been that close to a cow before and stepped back warily as it came across the stall. Then I noticed it had the most beautiful pale long eyelashes around its gentle brown eyes.

'This is Peaches,' Aunt Helen said, as she stroked the cow's neck. 'She's pregnant – but I don't think the farmer who dropped her off knew that. When she got ill, he was going to have her put down, but fortunately his neighbour, Steenie, is an animal lover and he was able to persuade the farmer to give her to me instead.'

'She looks OK now,' I said, although of course I didn't really know what a healthy cow should look like. 'Is she better?'

'Oh yes, although when she arrived she needed round-the-clock care. But yes, she's more than fine now and soon to be a mummy, aren't you?' Aunt Helen smiled as Peaches pressed her fringed furry head against hers for more strokes. 'Most calves are taken away from their mothers before they've even been properly weaned – that means they're still drinking milk from their mum.'

I nodded. Human babies got weaned too. That was when they started eating mashed-up food, when they weren't smearing it all over their faces or dropping it on the floor. Mum told me I was a nightmare when I started eating solid food.

'It happens because people drink cow's milk, of course. And sometimes the farmer wants the mother to have more babies to rear for veal or beef. It's sad for the calves, though. Can you imagine being separated from your mum?' I blinked. Aunt Helen suddenly looked awkward. 'Oh, sorry. I didn't mean –'

But it was OK. I *did* know what it felt like to have your parents far away. It felt very unfair and a bit lonely. I had the strange feeling that I wanted to give Peaches a stroke, but Aunt Helen was doing it already and so gently that I didn't want to interrupt.

'When your calf is born it will never be taken away,' Aunt Helen whispered to the cow.

Peaches looked over at me and gave another, softer, moo.

'You can stroke her too if you like,' Aunt Helen said, giving Peaches' nose a kiss.

Now I felt nervous. Those horns looked sharp and what if Peaches bit me? I knew cows eat grass, of course. Everyone knows that. But they still have teeth.

'Aren't you frightened she might injure you?' I asked Aunt Helen.

Even if Peaches stepped on Aunt Helen's foot accidentally she could do a lot of damage.

Aunt Helen shook her head. 'Not at all.'

I reached out and gave Peaches a quick pat on the neck. She felt soft and warm.

'Come on,' said Aunt Helen. 'Let's say hello to Jock the goat next. Though I doubt he'll say hello back!'

I followed Aunt Helen and Mackenzie to a hay-strewn stall close by. At first I thought it was empty. Could Jock have run off? But then I spotted a shape facing away from us, lying partly hidden by a mound of hay, his head resting on the ground. Without even seeing Jock's face, I could tell he was miserable.

'I'm really worried about him,' Aunt Helen said. 'Jock, Jock!' But Jock didn't even raise his head. It was as if he hadn't heard her at all.

'Is he sick?' I asked.

Aunt Helen sighed and shook her head. 'Sheena can't find anything wrong with him but he's hardly eaten anything since he arrived a few days ago. He won't even go outside, although the paddock door leading from his stall is always left open for him during the day. It's like he's . . . he's just . . .'

'Sad,' I said. 'He looks sad.' If there was ever a blue goat it was Jock. I didn't know a thing about goats, but I knew a thing or two about feeling sad.

Aunt Helen bit her bottom lip. 'He used to live with a sheep in a tiny field that was more mud than grass. The owner's son said he'd keep the sheep but couldn't look after Jock as well and so he asked if I'd take him on.'

'Maybe Jock misses the sheep,' I said, as I watched Mackenzie sniffing at a spot on the ground close to the wall. Could it be a mouse hole?

'You know, Mishka, I think you're right!' Aunt Helen said. 'Jock's missing his friend! That's an easy fix – the sheep must come here too.'

'What?'

Aunt Helen had only just been saying how the sanctuary was struggling and now she was planning to take in another animal!

'I'm going to phone and ask if we can take the sheep too. Animals form strong bonds just like people do, sometimes unlikely friendships. I'll do it right now.'

Aunt Helen pressed numbers into her mobile phone and waited. 'If we're lucky, we might be able to pick up Jock's sheep friend this evening,' she said with a grin.

It seemed to me that Aunt Helen could do with a course in business practice. Mum and Dad would never have got themselves in the mess she'd got herself into. They were always going on about how to reduce their taxes and improve their profit margins. I would have bet Aunt Helen hadn't even heard of profit margins.

While Aunt Helen left a voicemail for the sheep's owner, I looked down at Jock, who was still facing the wall. I hoped he'd appreciate the effort Aunt Helen was going to. But would the goat truly care two hoots where he lived as long as he had food and shelter? Was he really missing the sheep? Could animals have friends? I wasn't sure. I'd never really thought about it.

As we came out of the barn and headed towards a large shed Mackenzie looked over at the main house and gave a whine.

The barking that had been continually happening in the background ever since we'd arrived seemed to grow even louder.

Aunt Helen looked at me and I couldn't tell if she was holding back a smile. 'I think it's time you met the rest of the dogs,' she said, and I followed her back to the main house.

Chapter 4

Aunt Helen's paint-peeling, battered-looking front door had a large cat flap at the bottom.

'The cats like to come and go as they please,' she said when she saw me looking. 'As does Mackenzie. He's the only one of the dogs that's worked out how to fit through the flap!'

Mackenzie looked up at her and gave a wag of his tail.

'You didn't say you had cats as well,' I said.

'Do you like cats?' Aunt Helen asked me.

I shrugged because I didn't really know. I hadn't been able to spend enough time with one to judge how I felt. 'They don't usually like me much,' I said, thinking of Omar's disappearing cat that wouldn't let me make it a YouTube star.

'There's only two of them so far and they're very independent. Always off doing their own thing – apart from when it's food time – a bit like the tortoise! He's worked out how to use the cat flap too.'

'You have a tortoise!' I'd only ever seen one in a zoo.

Aunt Helen laughed. 'Yes we do. His name's Tommy and he's very independent for an OAP. I'm sure you'll meet him soon.'

Before Aunt Helen could open the front door, it was opened for us by a girl of about my age. She was wearing a washed-out sweatshirt and mud-stained jeans.

'There you are!' she said to Mackenzie.

'Mishka, meet Izzy, the sanctuary's hardest-working volunteer,' Aunt Helen said. 'Izzy, this is Mishka.'

'Mishka? What kind of a name is that?' the girl asked scornfully, as Mackenzie slipped past her into the house.

'It's like the streetwear label Mishka. You know – the one with the "Keep Watch" eyeball logo,' I told her. I tried a half-smile but got nothing in return.

Izzy was staring hard at my leather jacket. Maybe she was impressed with how good I looked. 'Is that fake leather?' she asked me.

'No.' Couldn't she tell quality clothing when she saw it?

'It's real . . . real leather?' she said. I nodded. 'Take it off.'

'What? No,' I said.

Aunt Helen sighed. 'Izzy –'

'I don't want him coming in wearing animal skin.' Izzy said, her eyes blazing. 'Take it off!'

I felt really embarrassed and wasn't sure what to do.

'Now!' Izzy put her hands on her hips and gave me a hard stare.

As I started to take my jacket off I caught sight of the label.

'*Fox* . . .' I muttered, confused.

Izzy overheard and grabbed the jacket from me. Her eyes widened as she looked at the label and the next second she burst out laughing. Loud hold-your-belly laughing, as if she'd just heard the best joke in the world.

'It says *faux* not *fox*, that means *fake*!' she said.

'I knew that,' I said, my face burning. But I hadn't really. I hadn't thought about what the jacket was made from. All I'd cared about was that it looked good. I took it back from her and stuffed it in my bag.

Izzy looked like she was about to say something else, but Aunt Helen cut across her.

'That's enough. Shall we show Mishka inside?'

Izzy stood back from the front door. She still had tears in her eyes from all the laughing as I walked into a dingy hallway with faded yellow wallpaper. Fortunately the dogs weren't right there waiting for me. They were in the living room with the door closed. Mackenzie was now sitting outside it. I could hear dogs panting and scratching from inside the room. Mackenzie looked at Aunt Helen, whined again and then looked back at the door.

‘They’re desperate for a walk,’ Izzy told Aunt Helen. ‘Been giving me loads of meaningful looks. I’d have taken them without you, but you said to wait until you’d picked up . . .’ She nodded at me and then added, ‘Of course, clever clogs Mackenzie let himself out by slipping past me when I went to get the dogs a fresh bowl of water.’

Aunt Helen looked at Mackenzie and smiled, obviously not the least bit cross with him. ‘How’ve they been apart from wanting a walk?’

Izzy’s face lit up as she told Aunt Helen about the dogs. It was almost like she’d turned into a completely different, much less angry, person. ‘Miss Lily’s been stuck in her chair as usual, ate about half of her food but wouldn’t touch the new biscuits. Darcy’s had a bit of a funny tummy – must have eaten something she shouldn’t have . . .’

Izzy went on and on and on, talking about dogs that I hadn’t met yet. I put my hand to my mouth to hide a yawn.

There were only a few barks coming from inside the room with the closed door now. It was as if the dogs knew they were being talked about. As if they were listening. Mackenzie was lying down next to the door with his eyes closed.

‘Do take your bag upstairs, Mishka, and then you can meet the dogs properly,’ Aunt Helen said. ‘Second door on the right just past my office – the door’s open, you can’t miss it.’

'OK.'

To get to the stairs I had to pass a room that can only be described as a paper junk room with a printer balanced on top of a chair – Aunt Helen's office. My mum and dad would have been horrified if they'd seen it. *A tidy home shows a tidy mind.*

As soon as I went into my bedroom, which was next door to the office, I knew it wasn't a room I would have chosen for myself. It smelt musty and looked like someone had just thrown it together. I put my bag on the floor and flopped down on the bed. It had an old brown knitted blanket covering the quilt and the mattress was definitely not as comfortable as my memory-foam one at home.

I decorated my room in our Edinburgh apartment myself and think it's just about perfect. It's got a photo quilt on the bed that I made myself. Took ages but wasn't all that hard to do. Last year I was really into photo transfers and made T-shirts with funny photos on them as Christmas presents for everyone. Omar wore his every day for a week.

On one side of my room I have a picture of my grandad and me at Cullen Bay. I used to love going to visit him in the school holidays and couldn't wait for the four-hour drive to get there to be over. Grandad used to have the picture up on the wall in his house, but when he passed away the picture got given to me. I think of him and how much I miss him every time I look at it.

On the other side of my room there's a poster of my favourite band and a rag rug I made in craft club on the floor. Under my window there's a tapestry window seat with cushions on it that I sit and people-watch from. There's always someone going by on the street below the window – loads of tourists. The Royal Mile's busy all year round and at night-time with all the colourful lights it's like I'm looking down at some magical world from afar.

I missed my own bed and my own things. The rug I'd made at craft club was a million times better than the worn one in this room.

'Ready, Mishka?' Aunt Helen called from downstairs.

'Nearly,' I called back.

I quickly unpacked my clothes into the old battered chest of drawers.

'The dogs really need to go for a walk soon,' Aunt Helen called up the stairs a few seconds later. They've been waiting a very long time.' Did she just expect me to throw my clothes into the drawers rather than fold them? Mum would have been shocked.

I didn't want to go downstairs to the dogs but I couldn't stay up here forever.

Aunt Helen met me at the bottom of the stairs. 'Ready to meet the rest of the family?' she asked me.

I nodded and tried a smile. It wasn't her fault my mum and dad had gone off to Japan without me, or that I was stuck here with her and nasty Izzy and a lot of dogs.

'At last!' Izzy said to me, when Aunt Helen opened the dogs' room door, which looked like it used to be a lounge. 'What took you so long?'

I ignored her. Then I gasped as the biggest charcoal-grey dog I'd ever seen in my life lumbered towards me. Its amber eyes stared at me. I backed away fast.

Aunt Helen looked from my frightened face to the huge dog and now I was *sure* she was trying to hide a smile. 'Oh, don't worry about Blue,' she said. 'He's actually a great big softie. Wouldn't hurt a fly.'

Which might have been true, only a fly could fly away if it saw Blue coming – I couldn't!

Izzy laughed. 'Kisses, Blue,' she said, and Blue trotted to her and gave her a great slobbery lick on the face and then another and another. It was gross.

Then Blue headed back to me.

'Aunt Helen!' I certainly didn't want any kisses from a dog.

'Sit, Blue,' Aunt Helen told him and the huge dog sat at my feet and looked at me. He had a trail of slimy slobber hanging from his baggy mouth. I tried not to shudder. How could Izzy let him 'kiss' her?

'What – er – sort of dog is he?' I asked. My heart was beating really, really fast and I thought I might need to sit down, only I was too scared to move.

'He's a Great Dane,' Izzy said.

'With a lovely temperament,' said Aunt Helen.

'Then –' I had to ask – 'why didn't his owners want him?'

Izzy looked furious. 'Because they're total idiots! He nearly died because of them. If he hadn't been found, he'd have been left stuck in that caravan to starve to death. He was trapped; there was nothing . . .' She swallowed hard.

'Fortunately he was found,' Aunt Helen said, putting a hand on Izzy's shoulder.

'But only just in time,' Izzy cried. 'He could barely stand.'

I looked from Izzy to Aunt Helen, hardly able to believe the horror story I was hearing.

'Was whoever left him to starve sent to prison?' I asked.

Aunt Helen shook her head.

'Lucky for Blue that you'd got space for him,' Izzy said.

Blue made a funny sort of sound in his throat as if he were agreeing with her. I was still more than a little bit frightened of him and put my hand on the armchair next to me. Maybe if I sat down he'd stop looking at me.

As soon as my hand touched the armchair it started to growl at me. I looked down and saw that as well as a hideous bobbled mustard-yellow cover and a blue-velvet cushion, the armchair had a tiny white-and-beige dog, with very shiny pink inner ears and pointed sharp-looking teeth, sitting in it.

'What sort of dog is that?' I asked, pulling my hand away fast.

'It's a chihuahua,' Aunt Helen said.

'And don't be deceived by her size,' Izzy told me. 'Poor Blue's terrified of her, aren't you, boy?'

I couldn't believe that! Blue was twenty times the size of the tiny dog.

'What's her name?' I asked.

'Well, we don't know her name; she was found wandering around the local primary school playground whimpering, but we call her Miss Lily,' Aunt Helen said.

'Because of her imperious nature,' said Izzy.

'Yes, she certainly seems like she's in charge!' I said. I looked at Izzy out of the corner of my eye – she seemed affronted that I knew what *imperious* meant and now it was my turn to hide a smile. 'Does she always sit in that chair?'

'Ever since she came here, three months ago now, she's claimed it as her own,' Aunt Helen said. 'None of the other dogs dare even try to sit in it any more.'

'Do you think she was deliberately abandoned?' I asked, thinking of Blue.

Maybe Miss Lily's owners had had enough of not being able to sit in their own armchairs.

'No, she was in too good a condition, too well fed, but had no collar,' Aunt Helen said. 'My hunch is Miss Lily got lost somehow. She might even have been stolen and then escaped.'

'Should I try to stroke her?' I asked. I thought I could be brave enough to stroke a really small dog.

'Only if you want to risk being nipped,' Izzy said. 'She can be very vicious.'

'Maybe let Miss Lily get to know you a bit better first,' advised Aunt Helen. 'But you can stroke Violet.'

Violet, it turned out, was a tan-coloured golden retriever with sad eyes.

'Why's she so sad?' I asked.

'Violet? I don't really think she is sad – not any more – not unless she was thinking about her previous owner. Violet was a much-loved assistance dog before her owner passed away.'

I steeled myself to pat Violet's head and she didn't seem to mind at all. She sat down and then lay down and curled up on my feet. It was like having a big warm rug on top of them.

'She must miss her owner,' I said.

'Yes, although dogs don't tend to live in the past, do they, Violet?' Aunt Helen said, and Violet looked up at the sound of her name and gave a wag of her tail.

A black Staffie with a white chest called Darcy had been given up when she was just a puppy because her owners had split up and neither of them was able to look after her any more.

'Some people can be surprised at how much hard work it is to have a puppy,' Aunt Helen said. 'They think it will be easy to look after, that they can leave it in the crate all day and it'll be fine, but it won't.'

Mackenzie came over and sniffed at my pockets. I wondered if he could smell the burger wrapper I'd stuffed in one of them and forgotten to throw away. Mackenzie put his right front paw on my leg and looked up at me with his big brown and blue eyes.

'What's he doing that for?' I asked Aunt Helen and Izzy.

'He's hoping you've got a treat for him,' Aunt Helen told me.

Mackenzie tilted his head to one side as he looked at me.

'Leave him alone, Mackenzie,' said Izzy. 'He doesn't have anything for you.'

Mackenzie raised his paw to me as if to shake hands. Blue stood up and went to sit by Izzy. He whined and Izzy seemed to understand him.

'All right, Blue, we'll be going in a minute.' Izzy looked over at Aunt Helen meaningfully.

I ignored her and talked to Aunt Helen. 'Mackenzie is such a lovely dog,' I said, surprising myself. 'And smart, too!' Smarter than a lot of people I knew. 'I can't believe his owners aren't worried about him.'

'Most dogs are lovely,' Aunt Helen said sadly, 'but that doesn't always mean they're wanted.'

'Some people think they can dump them like rubbish when they've had enough of them,' Izzy said angrily. 'I just –'

'Let's go for that dog walk now,' said Aunt Helen with a pointed look.

Izzy shut up and we traipsed out of the house.

Chapter 5

The dogs, apart from Miss Lily, who stayed in her chair, rushed excitedly ahead of us.

'See you've dressed appropriately for a dog walk in the country,' Izzy said to me with a smirk.

'What?'

'Maybe you should put on something not quite so . . . new . . .' Aunt Helen suggested.

'Or so smart,' Izzy interrupted. And that made me determined *not* to get changed.

'These clothes are fine,' I said through gritted teeth. Or they would have been if I'd been at the health farm my parents had led me to believe I was going to.

'How about borrowing some old wellington boots – at least they'll keep your feet dry,' Aunt Helen said.

I looked down at my cream canvas retros.

'No thanks,' I said.

I really didn't want to wear a pair of old wellies. I didn't want to wear what they were wearing. I wanted to wear my own clothes and my own shoes. I wanted to be myself.

But I knew almost as soon as we stepped into the field at the back of the sanctuary that I should have accepted Aunt Helen's offer. In less than a minute my canvas shoes were completely ruined and my feet were soaked as I squelched though the soggy mud.

I saw Izzy looking over at me once or twice, but I turned my head away or pretended to be busy with one or other of the dogs when she did. It's easy to pretend not to notice someone looking at you when you're walking with four dogs, because there's always one of them beside you, looking up at you, hoping you have a treat or a ball, or just coming to say hello and have a sniff.

In the distance I could see some other people out with their dog. Then I realized it was the paint-spraying boys we'd passed on the way into the village.

Izzy saw them too. 'Maybe we should go the other way,' she said nervously to Aunt Helen.

'It'll be fine,' Aunt Helen replied.

'But . . .'

I didn't mind if we went the other way. I didn't mind if we went straight home. In fact, my poor shoes would think that was a great idea!

'We can't let them intimidate us,' Aunt Helen said.

The biggest of the boys was shouting at the muscular black-and-tan dog that had been with them before – Homer. I couldn't make out the words, but he raised his fist to it and I heard Izzy gasp.

The dog saw us and started to run in our direction. I didn't know what to do. Was he going to attack us? Should I turn and run? But somewhere, I'd read that it was better *not* to run away from a dog that was chasing you. I didn't run but I didn't breathe much either and I could feel my heart thumping.

Mackenzie looked at the dog and wagged his tail.

'Homer – come back!'

All three boys yelled and swore at the dog to stop but it kept on coming. When it reached us Aunt Helen's dogs wagged their tails and sniffed at him.

'Well, hello there, Homer,' said Aunt Helen.

Homer wagged his tail and sniffed back at Mackenzie, Blue, Violet and Darcy as if they were old friends. He seemed a big dog but I could see his ribs and I couldn't see the ribs on any of Aunt Helen's dogs. I kept my hands in my pockets so Homer wouldn't mistake my fingers for tasty snacks.

Homer liked Izzy and pushed his nose under her hand for a stroke. She didn't seem to be in the least bit worried about her fingers.

Of course the boys didn't like us making a fuss of Homer.

'Get back here!' they yelled, and then added some choice words to emphasize just what they thought of him.

Homer ran back to them and they shouted some more.

'Do you think they're cruel to him?' I asked Aunt Helen.

'Negligent probably more than anything,' she said. 'That's why he finds his way over to the sanctuary so often. He's a smart and resourceful dog.'

'It's like the sanctuary is his own little takeaway,' Izzy told me, and Aunt Helen nodded.

'He's welcome any time,' she said. 'I don't like to think of him being hungry.'

It had started to rain and though I hoped it might make Aunt Helen turn back, she persevered. She said the dogs didn't mind a few spits of rain and neither should we.

'Some of them will be a lot wetter after they've been for a swim in the river.'

I was worried that we were getting even closer to the gang of boys but they started to move on – maybe the rain was good for something after all.

'At least it'll come out in the wash,' Aunt Helen said.

'What will?' I asked her.

'The mud on your jeans.'

But that wasn't the point. They were never going to look as good after this.

And then, worse, as we were going through a particularly muddy bit I slipped and landed on my backside. Hard.

Mackenzie gave me a lick on the side of my face and I squeaked in terror thinking he was going to bite me. But he just gave me a big doggy grin instead.

'Are you OK?' Aunt Helen asked, as I scrambled to my feet.

No, I wanted to say. *Not at all.* But then I caught Izzy trying hard not to laugh, so what I said out loud was, 'Fine.' I couldn't believe this day hadn't ended yet.

It was even muddier at the riverbank but the dogs were very excited to be there and kept running around Izzy and Aunt Helen.

'All right, all right.' Aunt Helen laughed, and she pulled a ball from her jacket pocket. Darcy immediately sat down. 'Ready, Darcy?' she said.

I'm pretty sure if Darcy could speak the Staffie would have said, Yes – ready and waiting!

The next second Aunt Helen threw the ball into the river and Darcy leapt in after it, swam to the ball, grabbed it in her mouth and then turned and swam back again.

'We used to throw sticks but they can be dangerous and damage a dog's mouth or get caught in their throat, so now we always bring a ball instead,' Aunt Helen told me, as Darcy reached the river's edge and came over to her.

The Staffie dropped the ball at her feet, wagged her tail, looked down at the ball, then up at Aunt Helen and then down at the ball again. Darcy didn't need words – it was crystal clear what she wanted.

'Why don't you throw the ball for her, Mishka?' Aunt Helen said.

'Oh no, it's OK,' I said.

Darcy had had the ball in her mouth and it'd be covered with her slobber.

'Go on,' Izzy said. 'Darcy's waiting.'

And Darcy was waiting, while wagging her tail and looking at each of us, pleading with her eyes. I picked it up and threw it at the river. It didn't go very far.

'That's not much of a throw,' said Izzy.

But Darcy didn't seem to mind. She jumped into the river, got the ball in her mouth and then swam around with it for a bit before swimming back to the bank. Only this time when she reached the riverbank Mackenzie grabbed the ball in his mouth and ran back with it.

'Oh, now you want to play, do you?' Izzy said, and she threw the ball far into the river and both Darcy and Mackenzie swam out to get it. Darcy reached the ball first and swam back triumphant, with Mackenzie close behind her.

‘Darcy, stop it!’ I squealed, as the dog shook herself dry next to me.

Darcy dropped the ball at my feet and gave me a look as if to say, ‘What’s the fuss about?’ Then she looked down at the ball and up at me.

This time when I threw it, it went much further.

Violet barked as Darcy and Mackenzie jumped in and out of the water. It was as if she was saying be careful, or perhaps she really wanted to play but wasn’t quite brave enough to join in.

The dogs had a great play by themselves, chasing after the ball by the riverbank. Aunt Helen and Izzy looked on and laughed and encouraged them as if they were in no hurry and had all the time in the world. Meanwhile I just stood there in my muddy jeans and ruined canvas shoes, shivering because I didn’t have my jacket and my feet were soaked.

We were almost back at the house when an old lady with a lot of long wild-looking grey hair hailed us. ‘Had a nice walk then?’

‘Yes thank you, Mrs Enders,’ Aunt Helen called back. ‘This is my nephew Mishka. He’s staying with me for a little while, so don’t be concerned if you see him about.’

The old woman looked at me with one eyebrow raised. ‘Looks like you could do with some country clothes,’ she told me.

I was too cold and wet to do more than nod in reply.

'Mrs Enders owns the place next door,' Aunt Helen told me as I squelched onwards.

By the time we got back to Aunt Helen's house, I knew without a doubt that my jeans were totally ruined. I might as well throw them away. Izzy looked at me and shrugged as if to say, 'We did warn you.' I thought I couldn't hate anyone any more than I hated Izzy at that moment.

This would never have happened if my parents had taken me with them to Japan!

Chapter 6

Aunt Helen and Izzy got busy towel-drying the wet dogs. I stood looking on and shivering.

'Why don't you change your clothes and have a hot shower, Mishka?' Aunt Helen said.

I didn't need to be asked twice and raced up the stairs.

The hot water felt *soooo* good and took all the mud away from me at least. But no amount of washing powder would save my canvas retros.

The burger wrapper in my jeans pocket had disintegrated into pulp. Luckily my phone was safely in my jacket hanging up in the wardrobe. I pulled it from the pocket and saw I'd missed a text from Mum and Dad.

Hope all good with you. Left Helsinki, next stop Tokyo! xxx

When I'd dried myself on one of Aunt Helen's old towels, put on some fresh clothes and warmed up a bit, I headed downstairs. Izzy had gone home. Good. I hoped she wasn't going to come back.

'Izzy's been a great help,' Aunt Helen said. 'Sometimes I don't know what I'd do without her. It's amazing how much time looking after the animals takes.'

This didn't sound good. I'd been hoping not to have to see her again.

'The days just disappear,' Aunt Helen continued. 'And there's really no time for anything else. I can't keep up with all the paperwork and the admin side of things is a nightmare.'

I knew that from her office that I'd peeped into – what a mess!

'How often does Izzy come to help?' I asked. I tried to make it sound like I didn't much care, but Aunt Helen gave me a funny look.

'All the time really, every weekend and after school, sometimes even before school, and now it's the holidays she's here even more. I've had a few volunteers that help occasionally, and dear Steenie's very good if I have an emergency, but Izzy's probably the most devoted and definitely comes the most often. I wish I could pay her but I just don't have enough money to do so. I can't even pay myself! Not that I care about that. The animals are much more important than money . . .'

Only she needed money too of course, if this place was to survive. I resisted telling her my mum and dad always say that money makes the world go round.

'Would you like to see the rest of the property before we feed the dogs?' Aunt Helen asked.

I nodded and we set off with Blue, Violet, Darcy and Mackenzie following us. Miss Lily stayed in her armchair.

As well as the main house and the barn where Peaches and Jock the goat lived, Aunt Helen had a paved yard at the front of the house, a huge garden behind it, a field, a pond and three sheds – two smaller ones, one of which she kept chickens in, and one huge one.

'When I bought this place with the money your grandfather left me I had such plans,' she said. 'But everything takes time, and money, and both of those seem to be in short supply.'

I thought about the money that Grandad had left me too. I knew it was a lot – only I couldn't spend it yet, or at least not unless my mum and dad signed some forms to say I could. The money had been put in trust until I was eighteen – still six years away.

I was looking forward to spending it one day, though, and had loads of continually changing plans for it. Sometimes I thought I'd use the money to travel round the world. Other times I wanted to use it to launch myself as an artist or rent a studio. I would have gladly used some of it to pay to go to Japan with my parents – if they'd only let me!

I stopped thinking about my inheritance money when Aunt Helen pulled the doors of the largest shed open. Inside it was dirty and dusty. Near the door there was a lawnmower that looked so old it could have been sold as an antique.

In one corner stood a large wooden horse cart full of woodworm. It had two long wooden poles for attaching it to the horse's harness and looked pretty heavy to pull. Then there were shovels and forks, and further back in the shed there were what looked like broken parts of tractors and other farm machinery. A broken gate and planks of wood. Even an old bathtub and a pile of newspapers along with a giant roll of chicken wire. There was so much junk lying about I was pretty sure Aunt Helen couldn't have known half of what she had.

'All of this stuff was in the shed when I bought the place,' she said. 'One day I'll get round to getting rid of it. I used to think I could make this a specialized dog training centre. So many of the dogs I see have so much untapped potential to make a huge difference to people's lives.'

'Like guide dogs?' I said.

'Guide dogs are probably the most well known of the assistance dogs. But there are also dogs that help people with hearing loss and other disabilities, like mobility problems or epilepsy or even diabetes.'

'Like Violet used to do?'

Aunt Helen nodded. 'Some dogs visit people in hospitals – some even go into schools to help children practise their reading.'

'But dogs can't read!' I said.

Aunt Helen shook her head. 'Not as well as you, maybe, but they certainly can be taught to read some commands and recognize symbols. And schools and libraries have found that getting children to read to therapy dogs is a great way to improve literacy. I used to take my old dog Logan into a local school. He loved visiting and the children were so excited to see him.'

'But they're – they're just . . .'

'Just dogs?'

I nodded.

'One dog I know can put the disabled person he lives with in the recovery position if he has an epileptic fit and then cover him up with a blanket! And family pets can do amazing things, too. One family I know is eternally grateful to their dog for saving their young son's life when he fell into a canal and the dog jumped into the water and pulled him to the side.

With a little training and encouragement almost any dog can help take a person's shoes and socks off – and find their shoes for them.'

'They can?'

'Or bring in the post, as well as finding keys and mobile phones. I even heard of a dog who goes surfing.'

I tried to picture a dog surfing in the sea. It made me smile.

The dogs in the shed, who'd been sniffing about while we talked, suddenly started barking and raced across the shed. Ahead of them was a mouse that scurried under a pile of farm machinery in the corner.

'Field mouse,' Aunt Helen said, spotting it too. 'Probably came in here looking for apples.'

I'd never seen an actual real live mouse before. It was tiny with huge black eyes and a golden brown coat with a white belly. Almost like a hamster. My mum hates mice. She says they live in dirty houses and spread disease.

'It's cute,' I said.

The dogs sniffed at the place where the field mouse had disappeared. Blue whined. Mackenzie started pawing at the hole in the machinery pile the mouse had gone into.

Blue barked.

'That's a play bark – they want the mouse to chase them now,' Aunt Helen said.

'Dogs have a play bark?'

'Oh yes – you'll recognize it soon. Everything's a game to them – and that's the best way to teach them. Play and fun – and treats of course.' Aunt Helen headed out of the shed. 'Come on now.' One by one the dogs followed her. Mackenzie and Blue came last of all. As he was leaving Blue looked back at the pile of machinery the mouse had disappeared into and whined.

'I know,' Aunt Helen said to him. 'But it probably didn't want to play with you anyway.'

I didn't know dogs could do half of the things Aunt Helen said they could. I'd have liked to have a dog come into our school when I was learning to read. It would have been much more fun than having to read aloud in front of the class or to our teacher.

'I thought I could teach the dogs that came here some skills,' Aunt Helen said, as we headed back to the house. 'So that if and when they leave they could make a real difference to someone's life. I don't *really* want to let any of them go, but whether they do or not it's good for the dogs to learn new things and be stimulated and praised for jobs well done.'

It was a great idea. So why wasn't she doing it? Aunt Helen had bought the perfect place for a dog rescue and training centre. All it needed was some work and more money invested in it.

'You could run regular dog classes to bring in money,' I said enthusiastically. 'Or how about turning one of the smaller sheds into a dog grooming parlour?'

'I'd have to hire someone to run it.'

'Maybe even have a boarding kennel. Or a doggy day-care centre for people who are out all day and don't want to leave their dog by itself.'

All Aunt Helen needed was a push to get her started – like me with my homework sometimes.

'And of course now there are the farm animals needing a home and tending to as well,' Aunt Helen said with a sigh. 'There's so much to do it's almost overwhelming but I couldn't turn them away. Each of them has so much personality. They make me laugh every day. But rescued farm animals don't bring in any money.'

'They could, though,' I persisted. 'If people visited to see them and hear their stories.'

'Would people really pay to come to such a small place?' she asked me, sounding doubtful. 'I don't have that many animals here and I don't want it turned into a zoo.'

Of course I didn't know for sure, but I didn't see why not, although she'd need more volunteers. And they couldn't be rude volunteers like Izzy.

'It doesn't matter that it's small. In some ways it's better, because it's more homely. Sometimes meeting lots of animals all at once can seem overwhelming if you're not used to them. But a few animals, friendly animals, coupled with the story of how they came to be here. Yes, I think I'd be happy to pay for that. People might even want to "adopt" an animal and pay to support it while it lives here.'

'You've got so many good ideas, Mishka,' Aunt Helen said. She sounded really impressed.

That only made me want to think of more ideas. Usually no one wanted to hear what I thought. I felt surprised and very pleased.

When we got back to the house Aunt Helen showed me what she'd been working on with Mackenzie.

'Take Mackenzie outside the door and push it to, so he can't see in, will you?'

'OK,' I said.

'Go on, Mackenzie,' Aunt Helen said, and he came over to me and went out of the door as if he'd been asked to wait outside many times before.

'Why does he have to wait outside?' I asked over my shoulder, as I followed him out of the room.

'Because otherwise he'd cheat.'

Mackenzie tried to peep round the door but I pushed it to. He gave me a reproachful look.

'Sorry,' I said. 'No peeping.'

I could hear Aunt Helen moving around the room and then she called out: 'He can come in now.'

I pushed the door open and Mackenzie hurried in.

'Find the keys,' Aunt Helen said to him in a happy voice, as if they were playing some exciting game. And, as far as Mackenzie was concerned, that was just exactly what they were doing.

He was looking all around for the keys. Inside shoes, under chairs, behind cushions. Every now and again Aunt Helen would say, 'That's it, find the keys,' to encourage him.

And finally he did find them – hidden under a magazine. 'Good job!' Aunt Helen said and Mackenzie wagged his tail like crazy. 'Bring them here.'

Mackenzie picked up the keys, which had a soft hedgehog key ring on them, and brought them over to Aunt Helen. She crouched down and held out her hand to him and he gave the keys to her.

'Good dog,' she said as she stroked him.

Mackenzie must have known he'd done well because his tail wagged and wagged and wagged.

'How does he do it?' I asked.

'I think it's mainly smell,' Aunt Helen said. 'I use the soft hedgehog key ring because it retains the scent better than metal, plus it makes the keys easier for Mackenzie to hold in his mouth – without it they might damage his teeth.'

'But, I mean, how does he even know he's supposed to find them and bring them to you?'

'Oh, I see. Well, I always use the same words and when we started working on "find the keys" I made them really easy to find by dropping them right in front of him and praising him when he picked them up. Mackenzie soon got the idea of what he was supposed to do.'

Then she showed me how Darcy could take off her sock if she asked her to. 'Obviously some people wouldn't want a dog who took off their socks. But it could be very helpful for someone with limited mobility.'

Darcy dropped the slightly soggy sock in Aunt Helen's lap.

Violet showed how she could carry a shopping bag and Blue demonstrated how he could turn the light switch on the wall on and off.

'It's not too much of a stretch for him to reach,' Aunt Helen said, as Blue switched the light on and off again.

I was really impressed! Just this morning I'd no idea dogs could have all these skills.

After the mini-demonstration it was time for the dogs' dinner. Beside the dogs' bowls on the floor there were full food bowls for the cats and an empty smaller one.

'That's Tommy's – I see he's been in while we've been out,' Aunt Helen said.

'The tortoise?' I asked.

'Yes. He was brought back to Scotland from Turkey after the Second World War, so he's very old, but he has no problems coming and going through the cat flap! In the summer I let him wander about where he likes. Once it gets colder he goes to sleep in the pantry for a few months and then lets me know he's woken up and wants to come out by knocking things over.'

I really hoped I'd get to meet the old tortoise soon.

Apart from Miss Lily, the dogs wolfed their food down. Miss Lily was much slower, but none of the others tried to take her food.

'That's why I think before she got lost somehow she was a much-loved pet,' Aunt Helen said, as we watched Miss Lily chewing each mouthful daintily. 'She's a dog who's never truly experienced being hungry.'

After we'd fed the dogs and made sure their water bowls were full of fresh water Aunt Helen set about making our dinner.

My belly rumbled and Aunt Helen laughed. 'Someone's hungry.'

It was only now the excitement of meeting the animals was over that I realized quite how ravenous I was.

A little while later Aunt Helen took a huge pizza with lots of Italian herbs, mushrooms, olives, peppers and cheese from the oven.

'That looks amazing,' I said.

'Help yourself,' she told me and I took a slice and bit into it.

'What sort of cheese is this?' I asked her round a mouthful.

'Cashew cheese,' she told me. 'Made from cashew nuts.'

Aunt Helen didn't eat any meat or fish or dairy. 'No good trying to save animals and then eating them!' she'd said.

I'd never had nut cheese before but it was so delicious I ate more than my fair share and sat back rubbing my tummy.

We were halfway through the food – well I was a little more than halfway because I eat fast – when Aunt Helen's mobile phone rang.

'Yes . . . yes . . . Well, I was hoping we could come now. Yes. No tomorrow morning would be fine. See you soon.'

She hung up and grinned at me.

'What is it?' I asked her.

'Jock's sheep friend, whose name is Woolly, is coming to stay!' she said, and she sounded as happy as if she'd won the lottery – which she hadn't but certainly could have done with!

Chapter 7

When I came downstairs the next morning Izzy was sitting at the kitchen table and Aunt Helen was over by the stove with Mackenzie at her feet.

'Morning, sleepyhead,' Izzy said scornfully. 'We've been up for hours.'

I gave a yawn in reply. There'd been another text on my phone from my mum and dad when I woke up:

In Tokyo now and at our hotel! Xxx

Tokyo was eight hours ahead of the UK. Weird to think Mum and Dad had already lived most of today and I hadn't even started it yet.

'Morning, Mishka,' Aunt Helen said with a smile. 'How about some porridge for breakfast? It's made with almond milk and I've added some local birch syrup.'

She put a bowl in front of me as I sat down at the table and I dipped my spoon into it.

I'd never had birch syrup before. It tasted like caramel. 'Mmm-mmm,' I said round a mouthful of porridge and I heard Aunt Helen chuckle.

'It is good, isn't it?' she said, and I nodded, as I dipped my spoon in again.

'Better go and see to the chickens,' Izzy told us, as she stood up from the table.

'Would you like to come and help collect Woolly, Mishka?' Aunt Helen asked me.

'Yes, please,' I said, mostly because I didn't want to be left at the sanctuary with Izzy. Although I wasn't sure about being left with the dogs either. It was different with Aunt Helen here too. I was getting used to the dogs and admired all their tricks, but I hadn't known them long.

Mackenzie gave a whine.

'Yes, you can come too,' Aunt Helen told him.

A short while later, I helped Aunt Helen hitch the animal trailer to the back of her jeep and once Mackenzie had jumped in we set off. It only took ten minutes to get to Ardarroch.

'This is Woolly,' a man with a beard told us while Mackenzie waited for us on the passenger seat he'd jumped into as soon as I'd got out. 'My mum bottle-reared her when she was a lamb and she'll do just about anything for a bit of bread. It's lucky you phoned because I wasn't sure what I was going to do with her. The neighbour who said he'd take her in has backed out and I'm needed back down in Gretna where I work.'

He gave me a loaf of sliced bread and I broke a bit off the first slice.

'Here, Woolly!' I said, feeling a bit nervous and not sure if the sheep would come to me or not. Who would have thought that sheep liked to eat bread – certainly not me. But then what did I know?

As soon as she saw me – though it might have been the bread – Woolly trotted over, ate the bread, then followed me up the ramp and went into the trailer as gentle as a lamb.

'Well done, Mishka,' Aunt Helen said, as I came back down.

No one at school would ever believe what I'd just done! I was like a proper animal person. A professional!

Aunt Helen lifted the ramp, closed the door, and once Mackenzie had jumped into the back seat we set off for home, with the bearded man waving us off.

Woolly hardly moved and didn't make a sound as we drove back down the quiet road.

'Are animals usually this calm in the trailer?' I asked Aunt Helen, as Mackenzie's warm breath ruffled the hair on the back of my neck.

Aunt Helen shook her head. 'I'm going slowly but even so most animals wouldn't be and I don't blame them. I'd be frightened if someone put me in the back of a trailer and then drove off, especially if I had no idea where I was going or what was going to happen to me. Even the bumps and twists and turns in the road are enough to terrify some animals and most of them have to stand up during the journey. I think us being calm – and the bread of course – has helped Woolly.'

When we got back Mackenzie and I followed Aunt Helen round to the back of the trailer with the loaf of bread to get Woolly out.

'Won't be a moment,' she said, as she pulled down the metal trailer ramp, walked up it and went inside.

Suddenly I heard the most bizarre sound coming from right behind me and almost jumped out of my skin with fright. When I peered round, Jock the goat was looking up at Woolly. The next moment Jock was in the trailer too and I could hear Aunt Helen laughing.

'OK, OK, yes, Jock, your friend's here. Now will you let us get out! Go on, Jock. Go on now. Woolly can't get out. You're in the way!'

Aunt Helen led Woolly down the ramp, closely followed by a very excited Jock, who also, as it turned out, loved bread. Jock was bleating all the time and once Woolly was down the ramp the two animals rubbed their heads together in greeting.

As soon as Woolly was inside Jock's stall in the barn she started munching on the food that Jock had refused to eat since he'd arrived and a moment later Jock was eating it too.

I looked at Aunt Helen and grinned, and she put up two thumbs and grinned back. Mackenzie gave a wag of his grey-flecked black-and-white tail.

From further along the barn came the sound of a loud moo.

'Don't worry, there's still some left for you, Peaches!' Aunt Helen said, grabbing what was left of the loaf of bread.

'Do cows like bread too?' I asked as I followed her. I thought they only ate grass and hay.

'Oh yes,' Aunt Helen told me. 'And apples and pears and carrots, corn on the cob and even popcorn!'

I stroked Peaches' neck while Aunt Helen fed her the bread. I felt much less frightened of the gentle cow than I had been yesterday.

'Her tongue's so long!' I said, as Peaches wrapped her tongue round the bread.

Aunt Helen nodded. 'That's it – all gone!' she told Peaches, giving her one last stroke before we headed back to the house.

Izzy had left a note saying she'd taken Blue, Violet and Darcy for a walk.

'Hungry?' Aunt Helen asked, and I nodded.

She made us salad wraps and we took them into the dogs' room where Miss Lily was sitting in her mustard-coloured armchair as usual.

'I don't like to think of Miss Lily being left here all by herself while the other dogs are out having fun,' Aunt Helen said, as she curled up in another armchair and Mackenzie jumped up and squished in beside her.

'It's so weird that my mum and dad didn't mention the sanctuary before,' I said, as we ate our lunch.

I'd always thought we were a family of non-animal lovers but apparently I was wrong. Maybe Aunt Helen's supreme love of them made up for the rest of us.

'I guess it isn't really their cup of tea,' Aunt Helen said. 'It isn't to everyone's taste. The mud and the mess . . .'

I laughed. I knew all about that!

'But they should have invited you for Hogmanay,' I said. Scottish Hogmanay, or New Year's Eve, celebrations last for three days in Edinburgh. 'We always have a torchlight procession on the thirtieth of December from the Royal Mile up to Calton Hill,' I told Aunt Helen. 'And then the next day there's a giant street party and everyone sings "Auld Lang Syne" at midnight. On New Year's Day some people go for a Loony Dook splash in the River Forth. The dogs would love that bit!' I thought back to last New Year and the party Mum and Dad had thrown. All their friends had dressed up to the nines sipping champagne and Scottish whisky.

'I couldn't have left the animals,' Aunt Helen said softly. 'And I wouldn't have wanted to even if I could.'

Now I thought about it Aunt Helen probably wouldn't have enjoyed the party. The money Mum and Dad had spent on it could have kept the animals here in food and bedding for months.

'Did you and my mum fall out?' I asked Aunt Helen. It was the only explanation I could think of for why my mum never talked about her.

Aunt Helen shook her head. 'We never really got on like some sisters do. I suppose it was because we just didn't have much in common. She was into her things and I was into mine . . .'

I thought I could guess what Aunt Helen's interests would be.

'Animals?'

She grinned at me. 'Yes. Even before I bought this place I had a beautiful German Shepherd called Logan.'

'The dog who came into the local school with you to listen to children read?'

Aunt Helen nodded. 'I wish you could have met him. He passed away just a few days before your grandfather did. Sometimes I like to think that the two of them are together now.'

Aunt Helen speaking about my grandad made me feel sad. Even though I hadn't seen him all that often because Cullen was four hours' drive away from Edinburgh I always loved visiting him. His house was really close to the beach and I could see the sea from the window.

'Logan used to love doing agility,' I heard Aunt Helen say. 'Before he got too old. He's the reason I'd like to run some agility classes here.'

'Agility's like obstacle courses for dogs, right?' I said.

'Right! But not only dogs can do it – you should see the chickens give it a go! Losing my dad and then Logan so soon afterwards made me take a long hard look at my own life and what I wanted to do with it. And then of course I met Mackenzie.' Her eyes shone as she gently stroked Mackenzie's furry back. 'Before this place I used to feel like I was just treading water – but now I feel like I'm really living my life!'

'We're back!' Izzy shouted as Blue, Darcy and Violet came bounding into the living room wagging their tails and flicking specks of water all over the place.

Aunt Helen looked at me and grinned as the dogs ran up to her for a stroke.

They looked as pleased and excited with themselves as could be.

'Yes, yes, I missed you too!' she told each one.

Violet's soggy furry head pushed itself under my hand for a stroke and I laughed in surprise and smiled at Izzy, who half smiled back, before biting her bottom lip.

'I've got to be heading off,' she said. 'I'm going into the village.'

'I'll make you a wrap to take with you,' Aunt Helen said.

But Izzy shook her head. 'I'm fine. I'll get something in the village. Oh – and I can't be here tomorrow.'

Good, I couldn't help thinking. It was better when it was just Aunt Helen and me.

But when Izzy had gone I soon found out that there were loads of jobs to do. The chickens, ducks, cow, sheep, goat, invisible cats and Tommy the tortoise needed feeding or food put out for them – as well as their bedding and water changed. Then late in the afternoon the dogs needed a second walk, which involved just as much mud as last time.

At least Aunt Helen made us a delicious spinach and mushroom lasagne for dinner but by nine o'clock I was falling asleep in my chair.

'Must be all the Highland fresh air,' I said, as I gave another yawn.

We took the dogs outside for a last toilet break before bed. The sky seemed much darker than it did in the city and the stars were crystal clear in the night sky.

'My favourite's the Dog Star, Sirius,' Aunt Helen said, as we looked up at them. She pointed it out to me.

'I see it!' I said.

It was the brightest one in the sky. I definitely agreed that dogs deserved their own star.

When we got back inside Mackenzie tried to go upstairs with Aunt Helen but she shook her head. 'No, you sleep in your room downstairs with everyone else now,' she told him. 'You know that!'

Mackenzie sat down and looked at her with his head tilted to one side. He put out a paw to Aunt Helen but she wouldn't be swayed.

'He used to sleep in my room, as did Violet and Blue and Darcy when they came here – but really there wasn't enough space on the bed and I think we all get a better sleep if the dogs sleep downstairs and I sleep upstairs. But it's hard to refuse them sometimes,' Aunt Helen told me. 'Plus I didn't like to think of Miss Lily downstairs all alone – and she wouldn't leave her chair for anything.'

It was hard for me to imagine sleeping in a bed with one dog – let alone four – and one of them a Great Dane!

'Night,' I said, as I headed up the stairs.

I'd got my pyjama bottoms and a T-shirt on and was just cleaning my teeth at the cracked sink in the bathroom when there was what I can only describe as a bellowing from outside.

'What is it?' I said, coming out of the bathroom and almost bumping into Aunt Helen who was pulling on a fleecy green dressing gown over her pyjamas and boot slippers.

'That, Mishka, is the sound of a cow giving birth!' she said, rushing past me and down the stairs.

Instead of staying in the warm I found myself running out of the house after my aunt.

It was freezing outside and I now looked enviously at Aunt Helen's fleecy dressing gown and slippers as she ran to the barn. Her outfit, although not stylish, looked so much warmer than a T-shirt, pyjama bottoms and no shoes.

Peaches was lying down on the straw and Aunt Helen knelt down and stroked her.

'It's all right,' she said, trying to calm the distressed animal. 'It's OK. Hush now. Ssssh.'

Peaches struggled back up to her feet, still bellowing, and a few minutes later Aunt Helen cried: 'This is it!'

Instinctively I closed my eyes and by the time I opened them Peaches was licking her calf clean. Underneath all the yuck the little calf was a soft cream colour.

Aunt Helen wiped the calf's mouth and nose on the sleeve of her dressing gown and it made a sound.

'Hello, little one,' Aunt Helen said to the calf. 'Welcome to the world.'

Peaches licked her baby's forehead.

The calf looked up at me, blinked and then sneezed.

'Look out!' Aunt Helen said, giving me a push. I just had time to move out of the way before Peaches released a stream of yucky stuff.

'Close call!' I said as the spray missed my pyjamas by millimetres.

'Just nature,' Aunt Helen told me.

The newborn calf was drinking milk from her mum now and making little sucking noises.

'You should call her Custard,' I said. It went so well with Peaches. The little calf was such a pretty colour with huge brown eyes and long eyelashes just like her mum.

Aunt Helen smiled. 'Custard it is.'

Chapter 8

When I woke up the next morning it was already raining and, judging by the grey sky, it looked like it was in for the day. At home I would have pulled the covers over my head and gone back to sleep. But here I knew the dogs would still need to go for a walk and the other animals would need to be fed and watered. Sanctuary life couldn't stop just because of the weather.

'How are Peaches and Custard this morning?' I asked Aunt Helen in the kitchen. 'And Jock and Woolly?'

'All doing very well, I'm glad to say,' Aunt Helen told me, putting a bowl of porridge on the table in front of me. 'Why don't you go and see them after your breakfast?'

I wanted to see Custard very much but I hesitated, not sure about going into the barn with the animals by myself.

'They won't bite,' Aunt Helen said softly.

Once I was outside I spotted some ducks waddling to the pond. They quacked at me and I laughed because it felt like they were telling me off for getting in their way.

Peaches was lying down when I stopped outside her stall. She looked up at me but it was Custard who came over and let me give her a stroke.

'Morning, Custard,' I said to the creamy calf.

I'd never even wondered what it might feel like to stroke a calf before. She was so warm.

Peaches gave a low contented moo and pulled some of the hay from the bracket on the wall beside her and began to chew. Custard went to see what her mother was doing but the calf was too young to eat solid food yet.

Further along, the two best friends, Jock and Woolly, were lying close together in their stall.

I hadn't really met the cats yet, or Tommy the tortoise, but I caught a glimpse of the tail end of one of the cats as it scuttled away, not yet ready to say hello. *Or become a YouTube star*, I thought wistfully.

Mum and Dad texted to say they'd been to a traditional Japanese opera known as a Kabuki. I tried to text them back, telling them all the stuff I'd been up to, but the rain must have interfered with the reception and wouldn't let me send it.

Are you OK? they texted later. **We're worried about you.**

Totally fine, I managed to text back eventually. It was short and to the point, but I was sure they would be really busy and barely pay attention. Plus they'd probably end up with loads of delayed texts from me tomorrow.

'The best thing about rainy days is snuggling up with the dogs in front of an open fire,' Aunt Helen said at the end of the day.

I was feeling very, very full from all the veggie haggis and neeps and tatties I'd gobbled up. Aunt Helen said the warming food would chase away the wintry weather.

I lay down on the floor in front of the fire. Violet put her paw on my arm and by now I knew she meant 'stroke please'. I obliged. It was hard getting up from the floor a few hours later to go to bed because it was so warm and cosy in the dogs' room and I knew it was going to be colder upstairs. Mum was right to make me bring a jumper with me.

'Night, Aunt Helen.'

'Sleep well, Mishka.'

I was fast asleep when my phone pinged and I saw another text from Mum and Dad.

Client meetings all day today. Text us ASAP! xxx

It was now pouring with rain again and I could hear the raindrops tap-dancing on my window. I thumped the lumpy pillow to try to make it more comfortable and closed my eyes. Nothing was going to stop me from sleeping.

I had a dream about my parents deciding to come back from their trip early and turning up at Aunt Helen's house unexpectedly.

'*We missed you so badly, Hamish.*'

'*Japan just wasn't the same without you.*'

I smiled in my dream as I climbed into the back of a white Rolls-Royce and the door slammed shut behind me, really loudly, which was weird because I'd have thought expensive car doors would close more softly.

And that's when I opened my eyes. It took me a second to realize that a real car door had *actually* slammed shut. It couldn't be my mum and dad, could it? They wouldn't really have come back from Japan early because they missed me so much, *would they*?

I scrambled out of bed and pulled back the threadbare curtains. Outside the rain was still having a party but I could just about make out car headlights – and they didn't belong to a Rolls-Royce. A man was out there over by Aunt Helen's jeep. He looked up at my window, and although I couldn't see him clearly because of the rain, I knew he definitely wasn't my dad. How weird. What was going on? It must be some special night-time delivery. Then the man ran over to his van and drove off.

I climbed back into bed and that's when I heard the sound: a mixture of a high bark and a whimper. I only just heard it and if Mackenzie hadn't started barking almost immediately afterwards, with the others all joining in too, I might have ignored it. But I didn't.

I ran down the stairs, opened the front door and went out into the rainy night. Through the mist of raindrops I could see that a puppy had been tied by its lead to Aunt Helen's car door handle. It looked like a miniature version of Violet.

'Oh, oh . . .' I said, not sure what to do. The puppy was so small and helpless. What was it doing here on this rainy night? It was getting tangled up in its lead and making frightened crying sounds. One of the puppy's paws now had the rope twisted round it so that it was hopping about on only three legs and getting itself more and more caught.

'Aunt Helen!' I shouted through the rain as I ran over to the puppy. But she didn't come out.

I'd never tried to catch hold of a wriggling, soaking-wet puppy before, and even one hopping about on three legs and tied to a car wasn't easy.

It started growling at me as I tried to help it and bared its tiny puppy teeth.

Then, as if things weren't bad enough already, a great clap of thunder exploded from the sky and made the puppy squeal and then bark at me as if it were blaming me for the weather!

I didn't want to get bitten, so I decided to untie the rope from the door handle rather than from the puppy. Much easier!

Only, on reflection, a whole millisecond later, perhaps not such a good idea when the sky was lit bright by a strike of lightning and the terrified puppy started running through the rain with the lead dragging along behind it.

'Come back!' I shouted, as I slipped across the muddy yard, but the puppy didn't listen to me and so I ran after it, now soaked through too. Fortunately, before I'd even reached the barn where Peaches and Custard were, the trailing lead led me to the puppy's hiding place behind the dustbins.

'Please, please, please don't be frightened of me. I'm only trying to help,' I told it desperately.

The puppy peeped out at me from behind the dustbins and then came towards me, its head low, its tail between its legs. It was almost crouching as it walked, as if it wasn't sure of the response it was going to get.

'It's OK,' I said. 'It's OK. You'll be all right. I'm here and I'll look after you. That's it, come on, that's it.' I knelt down and held my arms out.

The puppy had almost reached me when its lead got caught round one of the wheels of a bin and stopped it short. The puppy gave a yelp and sat down.

I jumped up, ran over to it and freed the lead from the dustbin wheel. It was a lot easier than trying to untie it from Aunt Helen's car door handle.

'There you are. You're safe now. You're OK,' I told the puppy, half to reassure it and half to reassure me.

When I finally picked it up it snuggled into me, very wet and cold. Through my T-shirt I could feel its little heart beating very, very fast and it was shivering.

'It's all right, it's all right,' I kept saying, as I carried the soaked puppy back to the house and pushed the door open with my hip.

'Aunt Helen!' I yelled from the bottom of the stairs. 'Aunt Helen!'

The puppy's big brown eyes looked up at me.

'It'll be OK,' I told it. 'You'll be OK.'

How could Aunt Helen still be asleep when all her dogs were very much awake – snuffling and whining and scratching at the door of the room they slept in.

'Coming!' Aunt Helen said, finally appearing at the top of the stairs, rubbing the sleep from her eyes. When she saw what I was holding her eyes widened and she came running downstairs. I followed her into the kitchen with the puppy in my arms.

'Who would have left it here,' I asked her, 'and *why*?'

'We may never know. Here, use this to dry him.'

She gave me a towel and I gently rubbed the puppy's soft fur while Aunt Helen warmed up some rice milk from the fridge to room temperature and poured it into a bowl.

'Poor little thing,' she said. 'See if he'll drink this.'

The puppy lapped up the milk with his tiny pink tongue and got rice milk all over his nose and whiskers. Milk all gone, he gave a big yawn. I knew how he felt. I was exhausted too.

'I'd better take him outside to do his business before he goes to sleep in case he has an accident in the night,' Aunt Helen said, watching him.

'I'll take him!' I said, as I lifted the puppy up and took him to the door. He'd been so cold when I found him I didn't want to take him back out into the stormy night, but luckily he did a wee as soon as I took him outside and I carried him back indoors. 'All done.'

While we'd been outside Aunt Helen had prepared a cardboard box with a towel and a puppy training pad in it. I knew I wanted the puppy to sleep in my room with me.

'Can he . . .?' I started to say, feeling embarrassed.

But Aunt Helen smiled. 'I thought you might want him in your room tonight. But if you let him on your bed, then don't blame me if you end up with a wet bed.'

'I won't let him on it.' The puppy could sleep in his own bed. But I did so want him to be in my room and judging by how he licked and licked my face when I picked him up the puppy felt the same way!

I carried him upstairs and Aunt Helen followed me with the box.

'It's best you carry him up and down the stairs for now – at least until he's seen the vet,' Aunt Helen told me. 'Puppies' joints can be very fragile and climbing up and down stairs isn't good for them.'

'There you are, puppy,' I said, as I put him in the box Aunt Helen had placed beside my bed. 'Night-night.'

'Night, Mishka,' Aunt Helen said. She paused. 'If you hadn't heard him crying – well, I don't know if he'd have survived the night out there.' She started to pull my door to. 'Thank you. Oh – and you might want to think of a name for him.'

Chapter 9

In Edinburgh I wake up to the sound of traffic. But at Aunt Helen's there was the noise of a cockerel crowing: *cock-a-doodle-doo.* It kept going on and on as if it were insisting anyone who dared to still be asleep should wake up.

I stretched and felt something warm and soft beside me. The puppy!

His mischievous brown eyes opened and the next moment he licked my nose and jumped up and then ran round the bed. I recognized the movement – he needed the loo!

'Uh-oh!' I jumped out of bed, grabbed the puppy, and got him on the training mat just in time.

'My grandad would have loved to meet you,' I told the puppy as he explored his way around my room. When we were walking on the beach at Cullen he was always saying hello to the dogs and their owners. 'Cullie,' I whispered and the puppy looked over at me and wagged his tail. Cullie was a good name for him – and Aunt Helen had said I could choose. 'Cullie!'

The puppy came running across the room to me and I scooped him up in my arms and let him have a play on my bed. He snuggled his little furry head into my neck. It tickled but it also felt lovely.

Then I heard someone outside my door.

'Aunt Helen?' I said. I couldn't think who else it could be but I also couldn't work out why she'd be scratching at my door.

I pulled the door open and found Violet outside, her tail wagging as she looked up at me and then behind me into the room.

Aunt Helen came out of the bathroom.

'What are you doing up here, Violet?' she asked the dog. But Violet was busy with Cullie. They were sniffing each other and making happy little sounds.

'We'll have to be careful which animals the puppy meets before we get him checked over at the vets,' Aunt Helen said. 'We don't know if he's been vaccinated.'

'I'd like to call him Cullie,' I said. 'If you don't mind – in memory of Grandad.'

Aunt Helen nodded her approval. 'I think that's a wonderful idea, Mishka!'

I carried Cullie downstairs with Violet right behind us.

When we got downstairs Cullie started chewing softly on Violet's ears and she was making a soft growling noise that sounded more like a purr. A happy growl!

'Here you are, Cullie, here's your breakfast,' Aunt Helen said, putting a small bowl down in front of him. Cullie gulped it down as fast as he could and then looked over at Violet's food.

Aunt Helen said he needed puppy food rather than adult dog food at the moment, so I crouched down to stop him from getting to Violet's food too.

'He could do with going outside,' Aunt Helen said, waving a plastic poo bag at me. I lifted Cullie up. 'Puppies don't take long for their food to go through them!'

She wasn't wrong and we'd only just got outside in the sunshine when Cullie did his business. I awkwardly picked it up with the poo bag, tied it up and threw it in the dustbin. Once we were back in the kitchen I washed and washed my hands with antibacterial soap while Cullie raced back to Violet. Before yesterday I could never have imagined myself picking up puppy poo. Omar would never have believed it!

When little Cullie fell asleep, mid-play, Violet lay close to him and watched him until he woke up.

'It's like something about Violet's changed,' Aunt Helen said, as she watched the two dogs together. 'And it's almost as if Cullie's known her his whole life.' She cleared her throat. 'Time for *our* breakfast! Do you fancy crumpets or toast?'

'Crumpets, please!' I said, my stomach giving a telltale rumble.

After we'd had our own breakfast we took Cullie to the vet's so he could be checked over. I'd never been to a vet's surgery before and I didn't know what to expect as Aunt Helen pulled into the car park of a one-storey building.

'Here we are! Sheena'll soon have you sorted out, little pup,' Aunt Helen told Cullie as I carried him up the slope after her and went in through the door that pinged as it opened.

A woman wearing a green tunic and a name badge saying 'Irene' was sitting behind a desk with a computer on it. To one side of the desk there was a closed door that I assumed led to the consulting rooms – just like at the doctor's or dentist's. There were posters with advice for animal owners on the walls as well as posters about different animal charities. One was for 'Give a Dog a Bone', a Glasgow charity that matched rescued dogs with older people.

Irene stood up as soon as she saw Cullie.

'Who's this then?' she asked with a big smile on her face.

Cullie wagged his little puppy tail.

'Hello, Irene.' Aunt Helen smiled. 'This is my nephew Mishka – and the puppy's called Cullie!'

'Nice to meet you, Mishka,' Irene said, as she gave Cullie a stroke and then lifted him from me to give him a cuddle. 'We used to have a dog just like you, Cullie. His name was Rex and he lived till he was sixteen years old and we miss him every single day. Our house just isn't the same now that he's gone.' She buried her face in Cullie's fur and he licked her ear. 'You are such a sweetie.' The phone rang and she reluctantly handed Cullie back to me so she could answer it. 'Take a seat but don't let Cullie on the floor if he hasn't had his vaccinations yet – just in case! We don't want him getting sick.'

'If he's microchipped and registered, then we'll be able to find out who his owner is,' said Aunt Helen, while we waited in the reception.

I looked at her, worried. I didn't want Cullie to be returned to the kind of people who would leave him outside in the middle of the night in the pouring rain. What if next time they didn't leave him somewhere like Aunt Helen's? What if next time they left him on a busy road? What if . . .

I was busy thinking of all the awful things that might have happened to Cullie if he hadn't been left at Aunt Helen's sanctuary when the door swung open and in walked a woman holding a very small rust-coloured pig wrapped in a bright red and yellow tartan blanket. A grumpy-looking man followed them.

My mouth fell open as I stared at them. I'd never seen a piglet this close before. The nearest I'd been to a pig was seeing them on YouTube.

'It was just there at the side of the road, trotting along on the grass as if it were out for an early morning walk!' The lady said breathlessly to Irene. 'We're on holiday up here, taking in a few of the Highland Games, but I couldn't just leave it, so I told my husband to stop –' Her husband didn't look too happy about that, '– and I picked it up, although I've never picked up a piglet before. It was very wriggly!'

Irene smiled. 'Little piglets can be as wriggly as eels.'

'She's always been soft when it comes to animals,' her husband said grimly, shaking his head.

The small rust-coloured piglet poked its snout out of the tartan blanket and blinked at us.

'Oh no!' the lady cried, as a spreading wetness suddenly started to trickle through the material .

'When you've got to go you've got to go,' Aunt Helen said, quickly jumping up and taking the piglet.

'None got on you, did it?' Irene asked the lady, who was looking shocked.

Her husband smirked. 'I did warn you,' he said. 'Fancy wrapping the beast up like it was a baby.'

'Actually that was a very good idea and probably made this little one feel much more secure,' Aunt Helen said firmly, and the woman looked relieved, though her husband's face turned sour.

'If it wasn't for you, that piglet probably wouldn't even be alive,' Irene said. 'Commercial pigs and especially piglets are very sensitive to the cold. They're not like wild pigs and boars that are much hardier.'

'But where did the piglet come from? Should we try to find its rightful owner?' the lady asked Aunt Helen and Irene.

Irene shook her head. 'Most likely it was on its way to the meat-processing plant. Piglets are notoriously wriggly and sometimes one or two do escape from the back of the lorries they're squashed into.'

'Meat-processing plant?' the woman said, looking at all our faces as if she couldn't quite believe it.

'The slaughterhouse,' the grumpy husband said. The woman's eyes widened. I felt sorry for the lady being married to him and ignored him when he glanced over at me for confirmation. I looked at the piglet Aunt Helen was now holding instead.

Cullie was very interested in the piglet and stood up on my lap and wagged his tail to say hello.

The little piglet wriggled in Aunt Helen's arms, obviously wanting to say hello back.

'Oh no, I don't think so,' Aunt Helen said. 'Not until you've both been checked over.'

A lady wearing a green doctor's coat and a name badge with 'Sheena' written on it opened the consulting-room door and smiled at Aunt Helen.

'We'll happily wait till after you've seen the piglet,' Aunt Helen said.

She gave the piglet back to the woman and the couple went in to the consulting room to see the vet.

'You'd like a piglet friend wouldn't you, Cullie?' I said to the puppy.

Cullie wagged his tail. I was sure he'd like to be friends with everyone.

Irene came out from behind her desk to give him another cuddle. Cullie licked her face and she laughed and laughed. 'You make me want to have another golden retriever so badly,' she said.

'We've got two goldens at the sanctuary now,' Aunt Helen told her. 'Six dogs in total.'

'Violet acts like she's Cullie's mum,' I added, and Irene smiled and then turned to Aunt Helen.

'I'm glad you've come in actually, Helen. I've been meaning to ask you if you'd be interested in a dog agility course I'm giving away? There's not space for it in the shed with all the collection buckets and cups for Lochmarron's first Highland Games as well. It's got jumps and tunnels, the works!'

Aunt Helen and I were already nodding before she'd finished speaking.

'We bought it for Rex ages ago but he took one look at the tunnel and refused to go in it or even go near the jumps – but I know lots of dogs love doing agility.'

'I used to compete in agility dog events with my dog Logan before he got too old,' Aunt Helen said.

'Oh, excellent. I'm glad the equipment will be going somewhere it'll be used. I'll drop it off later if that's OK?'

'That'll be fine,' Aunt Helen said, and she smiled at me and I grinned back because I was looking forward to seeing Mackenzie, Darcy and Blue doing agility. I thought they'd love it.

The couple came back out with the vet and the piglet and Irene handed Cullie back to me.

'Of course I understand that you can't keep her,' Sheena was saying to them. 'And even if you did want to, there's laws against keeping livestock in cities.'

'Maybe the piglet could come and live at the sanctuary,' I said to Aunt Helen, and Aunt Helen told the couple that the piglet would be more than welcome.

'Do you mean it?' the lady asked hopefully.

'Yes – we'd love to have her!' Aunt Helen said, and the woman smiled with relief and gave the piglet to her.

'I've been calling her Rusty,' the lady said. 'For obvious reasons.'

'Rusty doesn't have a curly tail,' I said. 'I thought all pigs had curly tails. They do in books.'

'Some do, some don't,' Aunt Helen said.

'Most commercial farm pigs have their tails cut off when they're very young,' Irene said.

'Do you think we might, on our way back, perhaps, come and see how Rusty's getting on?' the woman asked Aunt Helen. 'At your animal sanctuary?'

'Yes of course, we'd be delighted to see you and I'm sure Rusty would too,' Aunt Helen said, and she gave them her address.

'Time we were going,' the woman's husband said, ushering his wife out of the door.

'What will we do with the car blanket?' the lady said. 'We can't take it on holiday with us now. Could you use it?' she asked Aunt Helen. 'For the animals.'

'I'm sure we could once I've given it a wash,' Aunt Helen told her.

Irene put the tartan blanket in a bag and looked after Rusty while we took Cullie into the vet's consulting room.

'Come and have a cuddle, Rusty,' Irene said, and the piglet let herself be passed over as if she was used to being cuddled by people all the time.

The vet's consulting room was smaller than I'd expected it to be as I carried Cullie in. About the same size as a doctor's or dentist's, I suppose. Only there wasn't a chair or a desk for the vet to sit at. Just a counter along one side with shelves and a computer on it and a high, long table attached to the wall for Cullie to be set down on and examined.

'Morning, Sheena. This is my nephew, Mishka,' Aunt Helen said to the vet. 'He's the one who rescued Cullie!'

She sounded really proud of me and I felt my face going red. 'I couldn't have left Cullie out in the storm,' I said.

'Very fortunate that you were there,' Sheena told me, as she pressed a stethoscope to Cullie's chest. 'Very fortunate indeed for this little chap. He looks too healthy to be one of the dogs that were rescued by the SPCA from the puppy farm over at Strathcarron last night. I've been checking those dogs, mostly spaniels, over all morning. The inspector said they thought many of them had spent their whole lives in cages so small they could barely turn round.'

I cuddled Cullie to me. I was very glad he hadn't been forced to live in a cage and was now safely at the sanctuary.

Aunt Helen shook her head. 'It'll take a long time for those poor puppy-farm dogs to get over the trauma of being kept in a place like that.'

'The SPCA might be in touch to see if you could take one or two of them in,' Sheena said.

Aunt Helen nodded. 'Of course, anything I can do to help.'

I breathed a sigh of relief when Sheena told us Cullie wasn't microchipped. Now he wouldn't have to be returned to his original owners.

'I doubt he's been vaccinated either,' Sheena added. 'I can give him his first one today but he'll have to be grounded at the sanctuary until after he's had his second one so we can be sure he's properly immunized.'

Cullie gave Sheena's face a lick and she laughed. 'We don't want to risk you catching something nasty, do we, little pup?'

'I'm sure he won't mind being grounded – so long as Violet's there,' Aunt Helen said, and she told Sheena how the puppy and the older dog had bonded.

'And now Cullie will have a new piglet friend too!' I said.

I was really glad Aunt Helen had agreed to take on Rusty. You'd have to have a heart of stone to turn Cullie or little Rusty away, especially knowing that they wouldn't survive if you did.

Apart from the lack of microchip and vaccinations, Sheena pronounced Cullie perfectly healthy and full of life. At least whoever left him tied to Aunt Helen's car door had done something right.

Aunt Helen picked up Cullie and carried him back to the reception area where Irene put Rusty into my surprised arms. I could feel the piglet's little heart beating fast against my chest.

'Hello, Rusty,' I said, hoping she wouldn't wriggle too much or try to escape from my arms or need to go to the toilet again.

Rusty looked up at me and as she nuzzled her soft snout into my neck I felt my heart melt. She was so sweet and gentle. Maybe I did have a way with animals after all.

Now Cullie could reach her he gave the piglet a lick and Rusty made an excited little squee noise that sounded a lot like a laugh.

'I've just remembered there's a Games committee meeting tonight but I can bring that agility course round tomorrow evening if it's convenient,' Irene said.

'Thanks – how much do I owe you?' Aunt Helen asked.

'No charge,' Irene said. 'Not for the agility course or for checking over little Cullie.'

'Are you sure?' Aunt Helen asked.

'Certain,' Irene told her firmly. 'It takes a lot of money to run a sanctuary – especially a really good one like yours.'

'See you soon,' Sheena called after us as we left the vet's with the puppy and piglet.

'Don't forget your new tartan blanket,' said Irene.

I thought I was going to have both Cullie and Rusty on my lap on the way home but Aunt Helen said it was too dangerous.

'Both for them and for you.'

She nipped back into the vet's and borrowed a dog crate that we put both young animals into and bolted the door. Judging by the happy squees and yaps they made on the journey home I'd say they didn't mind at all.

As soon as we got home Cullie raced into the kitchen with Rusty running right behind him. Cullie gave a whine as he realized Violet wasn't there.

'We'll find her!' I told him.

I couldn't believe that just a few days ago I used to think animals couldn't communicate. Cullie's meaning was perfectly clear without any words.

Aunt Helen opened the kitchen door so he could run out into the garden. 'This way, Cullie.'

I watched as he ran over to Violet, who was lying under a tree with her head resting on her paws. As soon as she saw Cullie she stood up, her tail wagging, and Cullie raced over to her, followed by his new piglet friend. Violet licked them both and they cuddled up beside her in the summer sun.

Aunt Helen looked at me and smiled. 'How about some lunch?'

'Yes please! Only . . .' I didn't want to stop watching the animals.

Aunt Helen understood. 'I'll bring lunch out once I've seen to the dogs,' she said.

Apart from Violet, the rest of the dogs were still in their room in the house and barking to let us know not to forget about them.

Cullie yawned and then Rusty yawned too. In no time at all they were both fast asleep. I watched as their little chests rose and fell. Violet looked over at me every now and again as she too watched the sleepers. When Rusty cried out, deep in her piglet dream, Violet soothed her with a lick.

Aunt Helen came out with sandwiches fifteen minutes later. 'I've put some salad in Tommy's food bowl – he's very fond of lettuce,' she told me.

I still hadn't met the tortoise and was starting to wonder if I ever would.

Cullie and Rusty were still both fast asleep on either side of Violet.

'I'm not surprised,' Aunt Helen said. 'Sleep is how young animals process new experiences. Whatever adventures they had before coming here need to be slept on. Even with the older dogs I can take them for a long walk by the river and they'll still have lots of energy afterwards. But if I take one of them into town, or somewhere else new, with lots of different things to see, hear and smell, then they're much more tired afterwards.'

Cullie stretched and pushed himself even closer into Violet.

'Good girl, Violet,' Aunt Helen told the older dog.

I'd almost finished my sandwich when Rusty's little snout wrinkled and the next moment her eyes opened and she came trotting over.

'Uh-oh.' Aunt Helen laughed, as the little piglet stopped in front of me. 'I read somewhere that pigs have a very strong sense of smell!'

'Can she have it?' I asked, holding up my sandwich.

'Go on then – it won't do her any harm.'

Rusty made happy little nom-nom sounds as she ate the bread and peanut butter.

'I think she likes it!'

Cullie was still fast asleep but Rusty was wide awake and now snuffling about on the grass trying to find more tasty things.

'Shall we take Rusty to meet Peaches and Custard?' I asked.

'Sure – come on, Rusty,' said Aunt Helen.

Rusty trotted after us as we headed over to the barn, and Custard and Peaches' stall.

Custard was very interested in Rusty when I opened the gate to let the piglet inside and she dipped her fluffy head to give her a sniff as Rusty looked up at her and wagged her tail.

'Good girl, Custard,' I told the calf and Peaches gave a gentle moo as if she were agreeing.

I remembered worrying that Peaches might spear me with her horns or bite me when I first arrived. Now the very idea seemed laughable.

'I'd better get back to see to the dogs,' Aunt Helen said. 'They'll need a walk.'

'Is it OK if I stay here?'

'Of course.'

Not long after Aunt Helen had gone, Rusty started pawing at the straw with her little hooves, made herself a nest and then lay down on it. Custard, who seemed delighted with her new sister, knelt down next to the little piglet and went to sleep too.

Chapter 10

Izzy didn't turn up until late in the afternoon and as soon as Cullie saw her he ran up to her as if he'd known her his whole life, tail wagging, excited as could be, with Violet not far behind.

Izzy had a nasty-looking black eye. She caught Aunt Helen and me staring at it and buried her face in Cullie's soft fur. 'Who's this then?'

'His name's Cullie,' I told her, trying to avert my eyes from her bruise. What on earth had happened?

'Mishka found him – left tied to my car late last night, abandoned,' Aunt Helen said.

'Lucky you were here,' Izzy said to me.

'I didn't do anything that anyone else wouldn't have done,' I told her.

Izzy shook her head. 'That's just where you're wrong,' she said. 'Most people wouldn't.' And she actually smiled at me.

'That looks nasty,' Aunt Helen said, nodding at Izzy's black eye.

'S'nothing,' Izzy told her. 'Stop looking at it. Both of you!'

Aunt Helen gave her a look that clearly said, 'It doesn't look like nothing to me.'

'I'll get the dogs' food ready, all right?' Izzy said, and she disappeared into the kitchen. Aunt Helen shook her head and took Violet and Cullie with her to feed the chickens.

'I expect Tommy's over with them. That tortoise likes the chickens and sometimes sleeps in the chicken house with them.'

The elusive tortoise again!

I wanted to go with Aunt Helen and meet Tommy, but I was worried about Izzy. So I followed her into the kitchen instead. Izzy was busily gathering up the food bowls. I leant against the counter.

'What happened?' I asked her.

'None of your business,' she replied.

Back to her usual charming self, I thought to myself.

Izzy started to measure out the dogs' food into their bowls.

'Must be painful,' I said.

'Like you'd know,' she sneered. 'Had lots of black eyes, have you?'

'Nope.' I hadn't had any.

'Thought not.'

'Well, at least I'm not getting into fights like you,' I told her.

'It's not a fight if you don't get to fight back,' she said. 'All I did was tell Cyrus that if he stopped drinking cow's milk the spot on his chin might clear up.'

'You did what?!'

Izzy filled up the rest of the dogs' bowls as I laughed and laughed. I could just imagine his outrage.

'I bet he didn't like hearing that,' I said.

I took Miss Lily's bowl into the dogs' room and put it on the floor next to her chair. Izzy took the other food bowls outside to the paved yard.

'Dinner time!' I heard Izzy yell.

'Dinner time,' I told Miss Lily and she hopped off her chair and put her face down to her food.

'Nice?' I asked her, but she didn't look up.

As soon as she'd finished, Miss Lily hopped back into her chair.

I risked putting my hand out to stroke her but as soon as she saw what I was doing she turned round so she was facing away from me with her nose pushing into the back of the armchair.

'OK,' I said. 'Don't worry, I won't stroke you.' I put my hand down but I couldn't help thinking that Miss Lily, of all the dogs, was the one most in need of a stroke. She seemed so lonely.

I picked up a loaf of bread and headed out to find Izzy, Mackenzie, Darcy and Blue.

'Did you hear about our other new arrivals?' I asked Izzy, and when she shook her head I beckoned her to follow me as I led her to the barn.

Peaches gave a moo of greeting as soon as she saw us. Fluffy Custard came over on her unsteady calf legs and Rusty gave a squee of delight and hurried over on her short little piglet ones. I grinned as Rusty came to stand next to Izzy, who looked down and gasped.

'Oh! Oh!' Izzy said, her face beaming as she stroked the two young animals. 'They are so gorgeous. What are their names?'

'Custard and Rusty.'

I told Izzy all about what had happened last night and this morning.

'I never imagined in a million years that I'd see a calf being born,' I told her.

'I wish I'd been there,' Izzy said, clearly jealous.

Mackenzie wandered into the barn and came over to join us, and Izzy stroked him too.

'Custard and Rusty aren't the only new animals,' I told her.

We headed to Jock's stall. The first time I'd met him he'd been lying down and looking utterly miserable. But now Jock and Woolly headed over to us straight away.

Jock could easily rest his head on top of the wooden gate of the stall, but Woolly wasn't quite tall enough.

'They like bread,' I told Izzy, pulling a slice out of the bag I'd brought with us. I felt quite smug that I could tell *her* something for once.

As soon as Woolly and Jock saw the bread they started bleating and baaing. Woolly butted her head against the gate as if to tell Izzy to hurry up.

'OK, OK, it's coming!' Izzy said, as she broke the bread into four quarters and gave it to them. 'You weren't kidding about them liking it.' She grinned.

The next second there was a squee sound beside us and Rusty looked up at Izzy's now empty hands. I took out another slice of bread from the packet and shared it between the three animals.

I caught Izzy wiping at her eyes out of the corner of my own eye. Her fingers left grey marks across her face but I didn't tell her. It didn't feel like it mattered at all.

'I wish everyone could get to see what farm animals are truly like,' Izzy said.

'Me too,' I told her, as I bent down to give Rusty a stroke.

'Custard is so beautiful,' Izzy said, as she gave Peaches a slice of bread too. 'It makes me sad to think what might have happened to her if her mum hadn't come here. And as for Jock it's like he's a whole new goat now Woolly's here. Don't you just love this place?'

'Totally,' I said, as we headed back to the house.

Rusty trotted after us, looking pointedly at the bread bag. Izzy broke off a bit more and gave it to her. Rusty had just finished her second piece when Aunt Helen came back with Violet and Cullie.

As soon as Cullie saw us he raced over, his tail wagging excitedly, with Violet following behind.

'Have you taught him to sit on command yet?' Izzy asked me.

I shook my head.

'I haven't taught him to do anything. He's only just arrived.'

'Never too soon for a puppy to learn,' Izzy told me, pulling another slice of bread from the packet and handing it to me.

Rusty's little snout sniffed the air as if to say, 'Is that more delicious bread I smell?' I broke off a crust and gave it to her and then turned back to Cullie.

'Sit, Cullie, sit,' I told him, but he didn't seem to understand what I was talking about and started to play wrestle with Rusty instead.

I sighed and looked over at Violet. Maybe she could show Cullie what he was supposed to do.

'Violet!' I called to her.

Violet's gentle face looked up at me.

'Sit, Violet,' I said.

Violet sat.

'Good girl,' I said, as Rusty and Cullie stopped playing to watch what Violet was doing and the praise and treat she was given as a reward.

'Sit, Cullie.'

Rusty sat down and looked at me meaningfully. Aunt Helen laughed. I gave Rusty a bit more bread.

'You should video her on your phone,' Izzy said, and I gave my phone to her so she could do it.

'Sit, Rusty!' I said.

Rusty sat again.

'Good girl!' I gave her a bit more bread.

Izzy held up a thumb and kept on videoing.

Rusty chewed up the bit of bread, her face almost smiling as she did so. But it was Cullie I really wanted to learn how to sit.

'Sit,' I said again.

Rusty sat and so did Violet. More small bits of bread for them.

But Cullie didn't sit. He'd spotted a butterfly and ran off after that instead.

'He'll soon get the idea of what he's supposed to do,' Aunt Helen said. 'He's a clever puppy.'

But not as quick on the uptake as Rusty. As soon as I said 'sit' to Rusty the piglet immediately sat and then put out a trotter to me as if to say 'Treat, please.'

'I didn't even teach her that last bit,' I said. 'She must be copying Violet!'

'See if she can copy Violet when she does a "down",' Aunt Helen said.

Rusty only needed to be shown twice to get the idea that 'down' meant lie down, and in no time at all she could trot round me in a circle, and do a figure of eight by trotting round my right leg, through the middle of my legs and then round my left leg.

I wondered if all pigs loved to learn and were as clever as Rusty, or if it was just that Rusty was the smartest pig in the whole world.

'Are all pigs this smart?' I asked Aunt Helen.

'Some more and some less. The same as people!' Aunt Helen told me.

'Smarter than you, Mishka!' Izzy grinned.

'And smarter than you too!' I laughed.

Rusty followed us inside when Cullie and Violet did.

'Just don't let Rusty come into the kitchen,' Aunt Helen called after me, as I headed up to my room to upload the footage. 'And if you do, don't open the fridge.'

I stopped on the stairs. 'Why not?' I asked her.

'I was just reading the other day about someone who has a sanctuary with lots of pigs. She said that whereas a dog might wait by the fridge for you to open the door and get it out something tasty to eat, a pig, once you've opened the fridge door a few times, will be able to open the door for itself and get *itself* something tasty to eat!'

Izzy and I laughed and laughed as Rusty looked from one to the other of us.

'I wouldn't put anything past her,' I said.

'She's one smart piglet,' agreed Izzy.

Up in my room I played the video of Rusty that Izzy had taken on my phone. It wasn't half bad. A few minutes later I'd uploaded it to the YouTube channel I'd set up for making cat videos, ready for anyone who wanted to watch what a clever little piglet could do after a few minutes of training.

When I came back down again Cullie and Rusty were playing with the same stuffed toy.

'There's so many interesting things going on here all the time; we could have a documentary crew move in!' I said to Izzy as we watched the two young animals.

Aunt Helen had lots of toys for the dogs to play with and the room was full of them, most looking the worse for wear. As well as soft toys there were rope toys for tugging on, Frisbees and balls to catch, and Kongs and puzzle balls to hide treats inside.

'Helen says all animals need to play because it stimulates their minds,' Izzy told me, and I nodded.

Aunt Helen had even got a huge blow-up beach ball, still in its packet on a shelf in the barn, for Custard to play with when she was out in the paddock. And Aunt Helen had assured me that older cows liked to play too. The chickens even had a ball with treats in it that dropped out when they pecked at it.

Mackenzie joined in as Rusty and Cullie played with a velvety purple bug toy with extra long twisted-rope arms and legs and soft velvety antennae. The older dog tugged at it gently while Cullie and Rusty tugged for all they were worth. Mackenzie purred a happy growl as they played. Cullie made his puppy growling sound, while every now and again there was a grunt or a squee noise from Rusty.

'Mackenzie will teach Cullie how to play properly,' Aunt Helen said, coming out of the kitchen opening an envelope with 'Final Notice' written in red on it. 'So he knows to respect other dogs but also to not be frightened of them. Dogs that don't get to go out or be socialized when they're young can find it very hard to mix with other dogs later.'

'What about Rusty, will he teach her too?' I asked.

'I guess,' Aunt Helen said, but she sounded distracted as she unfolded the letter and pulled a face as she glanced at it. 'I've never had much to do with pigs before.'

Izzy shook her head because she didn't know either.

'I'll get in touch with that sanctuary I was reading about that had lots of pigs and see if they can give us any advice,' Aunt Helen said, and she tucked the letter into her pocket.

Chapter 11

It was after six when the doorbell rang and I went to answer it. Outside stood a huge man holding a bunch of slightly wilting flowers that looked tiny in his giant hands.

Not only was the man tall but he had muscles on top of muscles – like the Incredible Hulk. Plus he had long thick wavy dark hair all the way down his back and lots of tattoos on his arms and one on his neck.

I realized my mouth was open and closed it. 'H-hello,' I said.

'I'm Steenie,' the man said in a broad Scottish accent.

'Oh,' I said, staring like an idiot.

Luckily Aunt Helen came out or Steenie could have been standing outside all night.

'Hello, Steenie. This is my nephew Mishka. Mishka – Steenie. Let him in please.'

'S-sorry.' I stepped back.

'A'right?' he said, as he went past me and gave the flowers to Aunt Helen.

'Yep,' I said, as I closed the door.

Steenie was very popular with the dogs. Darcy brought him a ball and dropped it at his feet as soon as he went into the dogs' room. Mackenzie sniffed at his pockets hopefully. And when Steenie sat down in the largest armchair, Blue tried to climb into his lap as if he were just a small dog instead of the giant that he was.

Steenie laughed when he caught me staring at his muscles.

'Steenie's going to be in Lochmarron's Highland Games at the weekend,' Aunt Helen told me.

'Hey, Steenie,' said Izzy, coming in from outside where she'd been feeding Jock and Woolly. Rusty was right behind her, no doubt to help pick up any dropped bits. 'How's the training going?'

Steenie raised one of his arms in classic body builder pose to show Izzy how his training was going. Now his muscles looked the size of footballs!

'Pretty good. Been working on pulling a tractor today,' he said.

'A tractor?' I asked.

'Yes – to build up my strength. I'll be lifting a smiddy stane and walking with it as far as I can across the playing field on Saturday.'

'It weighs 165 kilograms,' Izzy said. 'In the olden days the blacksmiths used the heavy stone to tether the horses they were making shoes for.'

'Will you be tossing the caber too?' I asked Steenie. I'd seen men in kilts throwing what looked like a telegraph pole up in the air on TV.

'Yes, I'm looking forward to that one,' Steenie grinned.

'Dinner's ready!' Aunt Helen called.

We left the dogs to themselves and sat round the kitchen table.

Aunt Helen dished up a curry and Izzy and I picked up our spoons and forks in anticipation. Steenie picked up his fork too. I thought he must need to eat a lot to keep all those muscles going.

Over dinner Steenie told us more about his training. 'This is the first year Lochmarron's taking part – so I had to enter!'

'There's over a hundred Highland Games held all over Scotland each year and hundreds more around the rest of the world,' Aunt Helen told me.

'I'd love to visit the one in Alaska,' Steenie said. I wondered if there was one in Japan. 'The press took photos of me tractor-pulling today,' Steenie went on. 'We need as much publicity as possible.'

'You could do with some publicity for this place, Aunt Helen,' I said round a mouthful of pilau rice.

I wasn't sure how Aunt Helen's animal sanctuary was going to survive without more money to support it. And that final-notice letter had looked ominous. We had to find a way to get the word out and money in.

That's what my mum and dad would do. Get lots of publicity to let as many people as possible know about their project.

Around me the conversation went on with Izzy telling Steenie about her confrontation with Cyrus and Aunt Helen telling him how we met Rusty at the vet's and Steenie talking about the Highland Games.

'I wanted to have a heavy athletes' float for the parade,' Steenie said. 'But –'

'That's it!' I shouted suddenly. 'The parade!'

They all stopped eating and stared at me.

'What about the parade?' Izzy said slowly.

'It's the perfect opportunity to publicize the sanctuary,' I said. I was really excited. 'I bet when people see the dogs they'll be queuing up to adopt them.'

'But Lochmarron's Games are this Saturday,' said Aunt Helen. 'We couldn't possibly enter the parade. There's not enough time.'

'Three days,' Steenie said, tucking into his second plate of curry.

'And we don't even have a float . . .' said Izzy.

'Not yet,' I said. 'But we *could*. That old wooden horse cart you've got in the large shed, with a wee bit of paint here and a nail there would be perfect as a float – and Steenie could pull it!'

For a millisecond Steenie looked shocked. Then he started nodding. 'Might just work. And we do need more floats in the parade! A heavy athlete actually pulling one would look pretty impressive.'

'We could have "Give a Dog a Home" as our slogan,' I said, thinking of the poster I'd seen at the vet's.

Aunt Helen shook her head. 'I don't know about a float. I've never been very good at crafts,' she said doubtfully.

'But I am,' I told her. 'I'm very good at designing and making.' And I'd love doing it too.

'But . . .' She still looked unconvinced.

Thank goodness for Izzy who backed me up.

'It'd be worth a try,' she said. 'It would be a really good way to let people know about this place and the brilliant dogs you've got that are looking for a home as well as the other animals. Who couldn't help but fall in love with Custard and Rusty if they met them? I bet most tourists have never been near enough to a Highland cow like Peaches, or any type of cow, to stroke one. And they'd love Jock and Woolly!'

But Aunt Helen frowned and shook her head. 'Not Custard, she's far too young to be in it,' she said. 'And I don't think Jock and Woolly would enjoy it at all. Although Rusty might – she's such a confident little thing. I'd be much happier for people to come and meet the farm animals *here* where they feel comfortable and safe than have any of the sanctuary animals stressed. Most of them have been through more than enough torment already.'

'Then why don't we have an open day too – the day after the Games!' I said. The parade would be the perfect opportunity to publicize it.

'An open day!' Aunt Helen said. 'I don't think you realize how much work would be involved. It'll be hard enough to prepare for the parade without an open day too!'

Didn't she see what an absolutely fantastic opportunity this was? 'The parade's like a giant free advertisement for this place,' I said.

'We could have collection buckets for donations,' Izzy said.

'I think those would have to be issued by the Games' organizers,' Aunt Helen told her. 'And we probably won't even be allowed to take part.'

'Any extra money raised is going to be divided among local good causes,' said Steenie round a mouthful of naan bread.

'Well, we're a good cause,' Izzy told him.

I nodded. 'We could have leaflets about the sanctuary that we can give out, inviting people to the open day so anyone who liked the dogs at the parade could get to meet them, and the rest of the farm animals. And maybe adopt them!'

'It does sound like a good idea,' Steenie said.

'Too good an opportunity to waste,' I repeated, staring pointedly at Aunt Helen.

'But it'll be so much work . . .' she said, running her hands through her hair. She suddenly looked very tired.

'Not if we all chip in,' Steenie said. 'I could get some of my friends to help. Tania's the most amazing cook. I'll text her now.'

'Yes – refreshments!' I said excitedly, as Steenie's huge fingers pushed buttons on his phone. I hadn't even thought of that. 'And we can charge for them! So we'll get even more money for the animals.'

Steenie had barely finished texting when his phone rang. It was Tania. She was really enthusiastic about doing the catering and she could think of plenty of other friends who wanted to help too.

No sooner had that call ended than Steenie's phone rang again. More people wanting to help!

I thought the time had come for Aunt Helen to set up a web page for the sanctuary.

'I can do it,' I offered. 'That's easy. But we'll need a proper name for the place.'

'Helen's Haven?' Izzy said doubtfully.

Aunt Helen shook her head.

'Helen's home for Unwanted Animals . . .' suggested Steenie.

But Aunt Helen didn't like that either. 'It's not about me – I don't want it to be my name . . .'

Mackenzie pushed the door from the dogs' room open, came over and rested his head on Aunt

Helen's leg. She stroked him and then looked up. 'The Paw House,' she said. 'For four paws and friends, although Mackenzie only has three paws. All animals welcome.'

'I like it,' I said, and Izzy and Steenie agreed.

While we talked I got busy drawing a map and little cartoon drawings of the animals at the sanctuary. 'Chicken Castle, Hoof Hotel, Water Wonderland, Paddock Paradise . . .' I wrote as I drew arrows to the different areas. The leaflets we gave out during the parade could have information about how people could donate money, goods, their skills or any time they could spare – even if they couldn't come along to the open day.

'I can make this look more professional and then print it all out on the printer in the office,' I said.

Aunt Helen shook her head. 'That printer's broken. I've been meaning to get it fixed.'

I bit my tongue, wondering how long it had been broken for. What was the point of having an office if you only used it as a junk room?

But then I thought about how much Aunt Helen loved the animals and wanted to help them. No wonder that side of things was neglected. She just needed some help.

'There's a computer shop on the high street,' Steenie told me. 'The owner's name is Kenny and I bet he'd do the printing for you if you asked him.' Then he looked over at the door and grinned.

I looked round too as Rusty trotted in. The little pig's snout pushed my hand and looked up at the table to see if there were any tasty leftovers. She must have got in through the cat flap because the last time I'd seen her she'd been in the barn with Peaches and Custard. Blue and Darcy came in after her and milled around us – not wanting to be left out. It was as if they wanted to be part of our plan.

When Izzy brought in Violet and Cullie to meet Steenie, Cullie licked Steenie's face and chewed on his long hair. The puppy looked so tiny on his lap as Steenie's giant hands gently stroked him.

By the time I carried Cullie up to my room an hour later, the YouTube video of Rusty had gone viral. I hadn't realized how many people, from all over the world, were going to be interested in watching a piglet learn to sit.

Hundreds of thousands of people had watched her and now they wanted to see more!

Chapter 12

Violet woke me the next morning with a bark outside my room. Cullie ran to the door and whined as I climbed out of bed, rubbing my eyes, and opened it. 'Morning, Violet.'

I carried Cullie downstairs to do his business with Violet closely following. He'd had a few little accidents in the house so far but fortunately not too many, and mostly they'd been on the stone-floor areas, which was good because they were easy to clean up – and I was the one doing most of the cleaning. My mum would have been both impressed and horrified!

'Violet raced upstairs as soon as I came down,' Aunt Helen said, when I came back into the kitchen leaving the two dogs playing outside in the sunshine.

She'd already phoned the Lochmarron Highland Games organizers and even though it was officially too late for us to enter, Irene from the vet's was on the committee, and they said they'd make an exception for the Paw House and we were welcome to take part.

'So that's good news!' Aunt Helen said.

When I told her how the video of Rusty was being watched around the world she held up her thumbs and laughed. 'She's such a little character.'

While Aunt Helen made us some breakfast I sketched out my idea for the float. Aunt Helen had said that all animals were welcome at the Paw House and what more famous Scottish animal to include than a loch monster? Not the real Nessie of course – we were nearly a hundred miles away from Loch Ness – but a smaller, friendlier one.

'Looks hard to do,' Aunt Helen said, as she placed a bowl of porridge on the table next to me.

I shook my head. Not hard but it would be time-consuming. 'I'll use papier mâché over wire to make the skeleton frame,' I said.

The truth was I was looking forward to it. There is nothing I like better than designing and making. Mum said when I was a toddler my favourite thing to do was finger-paint or stick things to other things. (Admittedly sometimes not always things she wanted to be glued together.) At school I'd helped create banners for the fete and decorated a table for the car-boot sale. I was sure I could make a float for the parade.

'Is it OK to use some of that spare chicken wire?'

'Of course it is,' Aunt Helen said.

'And if I could have those old newspapers in the shed too?'

Aunt Helen smiled. 'Glad to see the back of those!'

There was the sound of the kitchen cat flap opening and closing, and then a squee as Rusty came trotting into the kitchen. Mackenzie followed her in through it too.

'Well, good morning to you both,' Aunt Helen said, as the little piglet sniffed the cooking smells in the air and Mackenzie gave a wag of his tail.

I gave Mackenzie a stroke and Rusty the last of my now cool porridge, while Aunt Helen chopped up some watermelon for her.

Rusty thought the watermelon was delicious and snuffled it up and then looked pointedly at Aunt Helen.

'Sorry, there isn't any more,' Aunt Helen told her, in no doubt as to what Rusty was trying to say.

When Izzy arrived to look after the animals Aunt Helen and I set off for Lochmarron. It wasn't far and we could easily have walked but there was a donkey and a foal that needed to be picked up on the way home so Aunt Helen hitched the trailer to the back of the jeep and we went in that.

First we stopped at the hardware store to buy paint for the float. Then we split up to do our own shopping.

'Why don't you meet me back at the car in an hour? No need for you to be with me while I'm getting the groceries – have an explore around the village,' Aunt Helen said.

We'd just passed a clothes shop and it had given me an idea. Luckily the shop sold both men and women's clothes. Aunt Helen and Izzy weren't hard to find T-shirts for. But it took me a while to find a plain T-shirt in XXXL for Steenie and in the end I chose a vest because I wasn't sure his muscly arms would fit into sleeves. I used up most of the money Dad had given me.

'Oh, bandanas for the dogs!' I said, when I saw some on the half-price rack. I pulled out the money Mum had given me and bought what they had.

Next I went to the computer shop and asked Kenny, the softly spoken small bald man behind the counter, if he could print 200 of my Paw House Open Day leaflets.

'I'd have printed them myself but my Aunt Helen's printer's broken,' I told him, handing over my hand-drawn leaflet with the map on it. I'd decided it looked just fine hand-drawn, more in keeping with Aunt Helen's sanctuary than some glossy brochure. 'Could you print the logo on these T-shirts too?' I asked Kenny and he nodded. 'And some paw prints on the bandanas?'

'No problem,' Kenny said. 'So your aunt runs the animal sanctuary just out of the village? I didn't know it was called the Paw House.'

I nodded. 'You should come and visit.'

'I'd like to!'

I smiled. 'We'd love to have you. Now, how much for the printing?'

But Kenny hadn't finished speaking. 'I've been thinking of getting a dog – good company,' he said.

'Aunt Helen's got lots. How much for the printing?'

Kenny grinned. 'No charge. Not for such a good cause!'

My eyes widened. 'Thanks!'

As I was coming out I bumped into three people coming out of the shop next door.

'Get out of the way, idiot,' Cyrus said.

Izzy was right. He did have a terrible spot on his chin but I wasn't going to make any suggestions for how to get rid of it.

'Blind as well as stupid,' laughed one of Cyrus's sidekicks, the one called Donut.

I knew I was better off not saying anything, just hurrying away. But they were blocking my path.

Then Kenny came out of his shop and Cyrus and the other two pretended they were just hanging around and not causing trouble.

'I was thinking I could drop the leaflets about the open day off later if you like – the Paw House is on my way home,' Kenny said to me.

'Oh, yes please!' I said.

Kenny smiled. He didn't even seem to have noticed Cyrus, Donut and Jay, though I was all too aware of them glowering at me.

Maybe I should go back into the shop, I thought to myself as the door closed. But just as I was about to do so, Cyrus moved to stand in front of the door – blocking it. Now I was really stuck. I didn't know how Izzy had ever managed to be brave enough to stand up to him. I felt so scared I thought I might be sick.

Then a burly policeman turned the corner and came down the road towards us, whistling. Cyrus, Donut and Jay exchanged a look and then headed off. I couldn't help thinking, as I breathed a huge sigh of relief, that I'd had a very lucky escape.

'Morning,' the policeman said, as I hurried past him in the opposite direction.

'Morning!' I wanted to get back to Aunt Helen as soon as possible.

When I found her she had a present for me – a pair of green wellington boots.

'Thought you might prefer a pair of your own!' she said.

'Thanks,' I said, genuinely pleased and not caring a bit that they weren't designer. 'Here, let me pay for them.'

But Aunt Helen wouldn't hear of it. 'I want to buy them for you, Mishka. Let me – please.'

The boots were perfect and I'd put them on before we'd even got into the jeep and headed off to pick up the donkey and horse foal that were coming to live with us.

Chapter 13

'I'll be sad to see them go,' the elderly man said, when we stopped at the small cottage with a field out the back. 'Gertie's the last of my beach donkeys. I used to have five of them but those days are long gone now. Gertie hasn't been on a beach in years.'

'Did she like giving children rides along the beach?' I asked the old man.

'She never complained and never refused to walk along the sand,' he said. 'You're a good girl, aren't you, Gertie?'

The donkey looked at me with her wise eyes. The horse foal, who the man said was six months old, stood close to Gertie and whinnied.

'He's never more than a few metres away from her side. Named him Shadow because of it,' the old man said. 'He's good company for her and she for him. I still remember the day I brought him home. Gertie was sitting beneath the ash tree and the foal ran over to her as soon as I let him in the field. He was trembling like a leaf but Gertie blew soft air through her nostrils and he lay down next to her. By the time I came back with a few apples and carrots they were inseparable and have been ever since. It breaks my heart to be parted from them, but needs must . . .'

He helped to lead the donkey to the trailer and she went slowly with him up the ramp without any hesitancy.

'That's it, Gertie. Steady now, girl,' the old man told her as he patted the donkey's neck.

Shadow was a lot more skittish but he wanted to be with Gertie, so although he was quivering with fear he followed her up the ramp and pressed himself close to her.

'Gertie's used to trailers,' the old man said, as he gave her one last stroke. 'It's best she goes with you. Somewhere she'll be safe. Looked after. It's not like I'm getting any younger and little Shadow's not even a year yet. He'll see us both out.'

'You can always come and see them,' I said. 'We're having an open day on Sunday.'

'And if you can't come to that, you'd be welcome any other time,' said Aunt Helen. 'Any time at all.'

'I'd like that,' the old man said. 'Bring along a picnic lunch and eat it out in the air with Gertie like we used to do on the beach . . .'

Gertie looked back at the old man and brayed as we set off.

*

Back at the sanctuary I held the gate to the paddock next to Mrs Enders' orchard open as Aunt Helen steered Gertie and Shadow through it and rewarded them with carrots and apples.

Gertie nuzzled Aunt Helen and Aunt Helen stroked her. 'I hope you're going to be very happy here,' she told the elderly donkey.

The next moment all three of us looked over at the sound of a whinny. Shadow's hooves were racing across the long-grassed paddock. He ran round and round, shaking his mane and whinnying.

'Well, he looks happy!' I said.

Aunt Helen smiled. 'Yes he does.'

Gertie trotted over to Shadow as the foal lay down in the long grass and rolled in it with his legs in the air.

'We could put a few jumps in Shadow's field,' I said. 'Just so he can have a play sometimes.'

'Oh yes,' Aunt Helen said. 'He looks like he'd like some play things. I've seen a horse on the TV playing with one of those giant beach balls like the one I got for Custard.'

'I bet he'd love that,' I said, and I ran into the barn and grabbed the beach ball, still in its packet, from the shelf.

It took a lot of puffing to blow it up but I was determined and wouldn't stop until it was done. Custard and Peaches watched me as my cheeks swelled up like a hamster's. They must have been wondering what on earth was going on!

I took the ball into the cows' stall and headed out of their door into the field. All of the animals in the barn were free to come and go in the paddock or remain in the barn as they pleased during the day. But so far Peaches and Custard had spent most of their time in their stall. Custard sniffed at the ball as I headed past her with it, and then followed me outside with Peaches right behind her.

Shadow looked at Gertie, as if he were asking permission, before running over to Custard. He was obviously interested in the big beach ball too.

He jumped away as I rolled it to him, then came back to investigate it. The ball was so light that it bounced across the grass as soon as he touched it. As the ball moved Shadow went racing round the paddock and I watched him in awe. He was so impressive, like a perfectly honed athlete. While the foal went running Custard bravely headed over to the ball despite a loud moo from Peaches that I was sure meant 'Be careful!'

Custard put her head down to the ball and it moved off a little way and she followed it and put her head down to it again.

Shadow stopped running and watched her from the other side of the field.

Custard put her hoof out to the ball and it rolled further away this time.

Shadow looked over at Gertie, who looked back at him and gave a flick of her tail. The next moment

Shadow came running over to Custard and the two of them pushed at the ball while Peaches headed over to join Gertie.

Aunt Helen smiled at me. 'Animals are so amazing,' she said.

Shadow stood up on his back legs and pressed down on the beach ball with his front hooves. The ball gave a gentle hiss as it went down.

We laughed. 'Next time I'll get a stronger one,' Aunt Helen said.

'I think they'd like to play with a basketball or a football too,' I said. 'And they'd be much stronger.'

We headed back to the house, just as Jock and Woolly came out into the paddock to say hello to the new arrivals.

Chapter 14

Cullie was very excited to see us when we walked in through the Paw House door and licked and licked my face. Rusty kept squealing as she ran round in excitement, a little like Shadow had done in the paddock, but not nearly as fast.

'Get everything?' Izzy asked me, while Aunt Helen got busy making a lunch of veggie burgers and chips. Rusty trotted after her to 'help'.

'Yes – plus one thing I didn't want,' I told Izzy.

'What was that?'

'A run in with the you-know-whos.'

I told her what had happened.

'Stay as far away as possible from those three,' she warned me.

And I laughed because I didn't need to be told twice. 'Not planning to get close,' I told her.

'Good.' Izzy grinned. 'I tried Rusty on this while you were out.' She showed me an old four-piece wooden jigsaw puzzle with a little handle on each piece so Rusty could pick them up in her mouth. 'It used to be my baby brother's but he's six now and mum was throwing it out so I took it.

'At first Rusty thought the pieces were for chewing. She's very fond of chewing, as you know. But I showed her what to do by holding the pieces in my mouth and then placing them in the slots and she soon got the idea. Especially when I got some chunks of apple as a reward! She looked up at me and made little grunting sounds after she'd put each piece in, as if to say, "Reward now, please". In no time at all she was able to do the puzzle really fast without any prompting from me!'

It sounded like just the thing to put on YouTube!

'Did you video it?' I asked her, and Izzy picked up her phone.

She laughed. 'Of course I did.'

Aunt Helen and I laughed too as Izzy clicked play and we watched Rusty in action.

Cullie was snuggled up beside me but now he rolled over on to his back so I could give him a tummy rub.

'You should have seen Cullie when he tried to climb on Miss Lily's chair. It was just lucky it's much too high for him. Miss Lily was not impressed and turned her back on him. I think he'd have got a nip if he'd managed to get up there!'

Cullie and Rusty had made themselves a new special friend in Blue while we'd been out. Blue was such a softie that he'd let the little puppy and piglet climb all over him.

Rusty watched me giving Cullie a belly rub and then she trotted over, knelt down and rolled over on to her back with her legs in the air so she could have one too.

I thought back to when I'd first arrived and Aunt Helen had said how the dogs loved massages. I could never have imagined I'd be giving a piglet one but now it seemed like the most natural thing in the world. Rusty looked so peaceful, but I didn't expect her to fall asleep!

'She must be exhausted from all that learning this morning,' Izzy said.

I took the opportunity to run upstairs and add Izzy's latest Rusty video to YouTube. But when I came back my veggie burger and chips had gone.

'Where's my lunch? It was right there.' I pointed to the empty plate on the floor.

'You didn't leave it on the floor, Mishka?' Aunt Helen asked me, shaking her head.

I nodded ruefully. There was no way of telling which of the animals had eaten it because they were all looking as if butter wouldn't melt in their mouths. There weren't even any telltale crumbs.

Aunt Helen rustled me up a replacement lunch, and after I'd finished eating it was time to begin work on the float. Mackenzie, Violet, Rusty and Cullie came out to the big shed with me. Rusty was very interested in all the old wood and machinery that was lying around.

'No, Rusty, don't go up there – you could hurt yourself,' I told her, as she trotted up a plank of wood sloped against an old tractor tyre. She came back down when I waved a bit of apple at her, but she just started gnawing at the wood next to me once she'd finished it.

'No, Rusty – don't eat that. It could have nails in it.'

Rusty wasn't making it easy to get anything done.

Blue wandered in behind Aunt Helen when she came over. 'How's it going?' she asked me, and I told her, 'Slowly!'

Mackenzie, Violet and Cullie weren't being a nuisance at all. In fact, they looked like they were just about ready to fall asleep.

'Rusty probably needs a sleep too,' Aunt Helen said. 'Come on, Rusty. Let's go and see Custard.'

Rusty trotted after her out of the shed and finally I had a good look at the old horse cart I was thinking of using in the parade. Mackenzie, who it seemed had only been pretending to be asleep, came with me. The horse cart did look a bit ramshackle and I could see a lot of woodworm holes – but I reckoned it would be fine for the day.

I pulled on some old gardening gloves of Aunt Helen's, cut off some chicken wire with a pair of pliers and started to make the wire frame for the friendly loch monster's skeleton, which I would then cover with newspaper soaked in water and flour for the papier mâché.

I wasn't sure how Miss Lily was going to feel about her precious armchair being moved but I'd decided it would be perfect for the float. She'd look like she was riding on the back of the Friendly Ness as it swam across the Lochmarron loch. Aunt Helen said that often dogs are aggressive if they're frightened, and I thought Miss Lily was probably clinging to her chair because it was the only secure thing she had in her life. But we wouldn't need to move it until the last possible minute, and all Miss Lily would have to do was sit in it – the same as she did all day, every day.

I started to work on the cardboard waves, painting them different shades of blue. Then I cut up two more boxes and painted one white and the other green. *Mermaids and fishes*, I thought to myself. I could do some of those too and give the mermaids tartan tails and the fish tartan scales.

Mackenzie lay back down next to Cullie and Violet, and I was soon lost in my own little world.

'You're pretty talented,' Izzy said, making me jump. I hadn't heard her come in and didn't know how long she'd been watching me.

'Thanks,' I said. Today was turning out to be a day full of surprises. 'Which of the dogs do you think's most likely to be adopted?' I asked her.

Izzy shrugged. 'I'd adopt them all if I could.' She frowned and then added, 'But then I'd have to bring whoever I'd adopted back here to visit every day, because this place is the best! They'd miss Helen and their friends so much if they had to leave.'

I nodded in agreement. I wouldn't want to leave here if I was one of the dogs. But if no one ever left and went to new homes then soon there'd be no space for other animals that needed to be cared for.

By the time Friendly Ness's first coat of flour-and-water-soaked newspaper had dried, it was time for Aunt Helen and Izzy to take the dogs for their afternoon walk. I decided to stay behind and carry on working on the float with Cullie and Violet watching me. The second papier-mâché layer was ready to go on.

'We'll be back in a little bit,' Aunt Helen said, and I nodded, engrossed in my work.

They'd been gone for more than an hour and it was after four when the phone rang. Luckily I'd just nipped back to the house for a drink and given Violet and Cullie, who'd followed me, some water too.

'Hello?' I said.

'Do you take poultry?' the voice on the other end of the line asked me.

'We've got chickens here,' I said. *And a very noisy cockerel*, I thought to myself.

'Well, I've got two needing a home. I won't say where they've come from but I will say they're not looking good. Now will you take them or not?'

Aunt Helen and Izzy were out and there was no one else to check with.

'Whereabouts are you?' I asked.

'End of Summertree Down Lane. Barrow Farm. You can't miss it. Not more than ten minutes' walk from your place if you're sharpish. But don't count your chickens if you dawdle because they'll be gone.' He laughed at his own not very funny joke.

'I'll be quick.'

I left Cullie and Violet in the house and ran down the lane. I tried to phone Aunt Helen as I ran but I couldn't get a signal.

'I've come for the chickens,' I gasped eight minutes later at the red-faced, scrawny-necked man who stood at the gate of Barrow Farm with a basket on the ground beside him. A paunchy ginger-white-and-black cat came out of the hedge and slinked past at one side of him.

'And how much will you be giving me for them?' the man asked, staring at me with his sharp, birdlike eyes.

'Er . . .'

I crouched down and opened the lid. Two mostly featherless birds blinked and cowered away from me.

'Twenty pounds for the two of them,' the man said.

'I don't have twenty pounds!'

'Well, you can't just expect me to give them to you for free!' the man said, sounding insulted.

'I've got five,' I said, pulling out all the money I had left in my pocket.

'Chicken feed – but that'll have to do,' he said, plucking it from me as quick as lightning.

'What are their names?' I asked him, and immediately realized what a foolish question it was by his face.

'Names!' he choked out. 'They don't have names!'

I reached down to pick up the basket.

'You didn't buy that,' he said. 'You bought two chickens.'

And he pulled the birds from the basket by their necks and gave them to me.

'Good day to you then.'

As I headed back with a chicken under each arm it started to rain. One moment it was just *drip-drip* and the next, as often happens with summer storms, it was torrential. I didn't want the poor scraggly birds to get cold and wet. Had they even seen rain before or had they spent their lives indoors? Had they even seen daylight? What could have happened to them to make all of their feathers fall out?

I opened my jacket and put the two chickens inside it to protect them. They didn't struggle or try to get out, which I was glad of as I wouldn't have liked to try to catch them. But I was also worried. They were going to be all right, weren't they? They would still be alive when I got back? I ran faster through the rain that soaked my hair and got in my eyes and mouth. Usually I would have put my hood up, but now I had to use both hands to make sure the chickens didn't fall out of the bottom of my jacket.

I'd never been so pleased to reach anywhere as I was to get back to the Paw House. I pushed the front door open with my foot and ran inside. 'Aunt Helen!'

'Kitchen,' she called back cheerily, not noticing the desperation of my call.

Aunt Helen's neighbour, old Mrs Enders, was in the kitchen having a cup of tea with Aunt Helen when I walked in drenched through. The last time I'd seen Mrs Enders, her long grey hair had been wild and untamed. This time she'd got it in an elaborate, though teetering, bun.

On the table in front of them was the most delicious-looking cake I'd ever seen. It was made up of a myriad of thin multicoloured layers interspersed with fresh berries.

'You're always welcome to use the orchard if you need more space for the animals,' Mrs Enders was telling Aunt Helen. 'It's not like it's being used for anything else.'

'That's very kind,' Aunt Helen said, before both women stopped talking to stare at my wriggling jacket.

'What on earth have you got under there?' Aunt Helen asked me, at which point one of the chickens gave a pitiful cluck as if it were replying to her.

'He said they wouldn't survive if we didn't take them,' I said.

'What? Who?' Aunt Helen asked.

'I don't know his name. He lives at Barrow Farm.'

'And I suppose he charged you for them too, the rascal,' Mrs Enders said.

'Yes he did!' I told her, surprised.

'I'll see you get your money back,' she said. 'Shouldn't be taking advantage of folk, horrid man.'

The chickens both poked their heads out of my jacket. They looked at the cake.

'Can the chickens have a bit of cake?' I asked Aunt Helen. I was sure they must be hungry.

'Could give it a try,' she said. 'It doesn't have any eggs in it. Steenie's friend Tania brought it over for us to try and it is delicious. Though those two chickens might be too frightened to eat anything at all.'

But Aunt Helen was wrong about that. Our new chickens, it turned out, weren't frightened when it came to cake. They loved it! I crumbled it in my hand and they pecked away as if there was no tomorrow.

'Shall I put these two in with the rest of the chickens when they've finished eating?' I asked Aunt Helen, but Aunt Helen shook her head vehemently.

'They have to be introduced gradually,' she told me. 'There's a strict pecking order among chickens, and newcomers have to know their place.'

'They could do with some of those little jumper thingies they give to chickens without feathers to keep them warm,' Mrs Enders said, and I remembered seeing a video of chickens wearing knitted jumpers on YouTube. There'd been a tortoise wearing a knitted shell coat on the same video.

'I'll make them some,' I said happily. It didn't matter to me if I painted pictures, made sculptures, built furniture or designed clothes for people or for animals. Creating was the thing.

There was no time to waste and I took the two chickens up to my room to make their outfits. Behind me I could hear Mrs Enders and Aunt Helen talking about maybe extending the animal sanctuary into Mrs Enders' orchard.

'Used to keep sheep and lambs in there when I was a little girl . . .' Mrs Enders was saying.

Up in my room I set the chickens down on the carpet, hoping they wouldn't make too much of a mess, but it wasn't the same sort of worry as it would have been if I'd been at home in Edinburgh in our cream-and-white apartment. Aunt Helen's house was much more forgiving – and a lot more homely.

The two chickens were huddled together and didn't move a centimetre, although one or other of them blinked every now and again.

'Names,' I said, sitting down cross-legged in front of the bald birds. 'You need names.'

It seemed to me that chickens that had been through a trauma and survived needed glorious, fabulous names.

'Dolores,' I said, looking at the chicken on the right. 'And Aurora,' I said to the one on the left. 'Yes, definitely Aurora,' I said when Aurora blinked. 'Now to make you some clothes.'

The important thing was that I didn't impede the chickens' movements in any way. They'd had enough of that already. I didn't know how many chickens were kept in whatever cage these two had been in, but it must have been a tight squeeze.

Aurora and Dolores had to be free to flap their wings and walk about. I thought about the tabards the art teacher used to get us to wear for painting when I was a little kid. Tabards would be perfect and slip on easily over the chickens' heads. I needed to make them from something soft but hard-wearing.

And suddenly I knew what had to be sacrificed. My designer Christmas jumper that mum had insisted I bring with me just in case it turned cold. It had red and white stripes on the front, blue and yellow ones on the back.

Aurora could have the red and Dolores the blue. *Snip-snip-snip* went my scissors and in no time at all I had two chicken-sized tabards consisting of a head hole and two open sides.

'You look gorgeous,' I told Dolores and Aurora as I slipped their new outfits over their heads and knelt back on my heels to admire them.

They did look very smart indeed, even if I said so myself. I snapped pictures of them on my phone and then filmed them as they took their first tentative steps across my bed in their new outfits.

Chapter 15

I was used to there being more animals than people at Aunt Helen's sanctuary. But from six o'clock onwards it was the other way round as more and more friends of Steenie's turned up. All of them wanted to assist the Paw House in any way they could. I must admit I was pretty amazed and Aunt Helen must have been even more so.

Fortunately Tania brought lots more cakes and pies with her and Aunt Helen had tons of veggie burgers in the freezer. Steenie brought a crate-load of drinks and then phoned someone else to bring buns – and more drinks.

In no time at all there was an impromptu barbecue going on in the paved yard and Mrs Enders came over to join us wearing a long evening dress and her wellingtons.

Then Irene, from the vet's, arrived with her husband, Ray, and the agility course. Cullie raced over to them, his little tail wagging, with Violet right behind him.

'Oh, aren't you lovely? What's your name?' Irene said to Violet as she knelt down and stroked her.

'She's called Violet,' I told her, and Violet gave a wag of her tail.

Ray picked Cullie up and Cullie licked his face.

'And that's Cullie,' I told Ray.

Ray laughed. 'Nothing like puppy licks!'

'Where do you want the agility course set up?' Irene asked Aunt Helen.

'The paddock,' Aunt Helen told her, as we helped to unload the agility course from their people carrier.

'Come on, Violet,' said Irene, and Violet gave a wag of her tail and followed her.

Cullie was almost dancing along beside Ray.

'I didn't realize there would be so much!' Aunt Helen said, staring at what seemed like hundreds of pieces of the agility course that were now lying on the ground.

'Sorry,' Irene said. 'We went overboard. Is it too much?'

'No!' Aunt Helen laughed, and I grinned. 'It's perfect. But I should pay you.'

'Let's not hear anything about money!' Irene said, looking fierce. 'Not a word.'

Violet, Cullie, Mackenzie and Rusty watched as we set up the course in the paddock, with Gertie and Shadow looking on from the other side of the field. There were five fences that could be raised or lowered, a plastic tunnel to run through, an A-frame to run up and over, a bench to walk up and along and down, plus a see-saw for the seriously brave. Some poles for weaving in and out of, and a hoop on a stand to jump through.

'It looks amazing!' Aunt Helen said. 'Thank you.'

'So who's going to be the first to give it a go?' Irene said to the dogs that were milling around us, along with Rusty who never liked to be left out.

'No jumping over fences for Cullie,' Aunt Helen said. 'I don't want him jarring his joints.'

'That's all right, he can have a cuddle with me instead,' Irene said, scooping him up and hugging him to her. Cullie licked her face while Violet stood close to Ray and he bent down to stroke her.

'She's such a gentle dog,' he said.

'Come on,' Aunt Helen said to Mackenzie, and they ran over to the first jump while I got busy videoing everything on my phone.

'Over!' Aunt Helen said, showing Mackenzie what she wanted him to do with a wave of her hand.

Mackenzie jumped over the jump on his three legs as if he'd been jumping fences all his life.

Aunt Helen ran over to the next fence and he ran with her and jumped that one too.

He didn't look so sure about going through the tunnel, although he did peer into it. Aunt Helen ran to the other end of the tunnel and called to him. 'Here, Mackenzie, here!'

Mackenzie ran round the side of the tunnel to her and wagged his tail.

'Inside, Mackenzie, in,' Aunt Helen said, pointing into the tunnel.

Mackenzie looked up at her and then at the tunnel as if to say, 'Really, you want me to go in *that*?'

Aunt Helen pulled a dog treat from her pocket and threw it into the tunnel. Rusty gave a squee and the next moment she raced over to the tunnel and ran into it from the other end as everyone laughed. I kept on filming. This was too good to miss. A moment later Rusty emerged.

'Well done,' said Aunt Helen and she gave both animals a treat.

My phone started ringing.

'Hello!' It was Mum and Dad phoning from Japan.

'Is everything OK? We've barely heard from you!' Mum said.

'Yes, yes, everything's fine,' I told her. 'I'm in the middle of filming.'

'Filming what?'

'Dogs and pigs in tunnels! I've got to go.'

Darcy and Blue had turns on the new course too, while Violet and Cullie preferred to stay with Irene and her husband to be made a fuss of.

The agility course was very popular – some of the people even had a go on it!

'Come on, Steenie, over the jump!'

Steenie laughed good-naturedly as he and another Highland Games heavy athlete tried to squeeze themselves in and out of the weaving poles. I kept on videoing.

By the time everyone who wanted to had had a go, the air was full of the smell of delicious food cooking. As the dogs and most of the people – and Rusty of course – headed over for something to eat, I stayed behind to play back the footage I'd taken. When I looked up I saw Custard almost skipping over to the nearest fence and gingerly and carefully stepping over it. She looked at me as if to say, 'See, I can do it too.' Peaches came over to Custard and licked her daughter as if to say, 'Well done', before Shadow came running over and jumped over all of the fences as if they were no more than stepping stones. And then for good measure he did it all again!

I felt something move by my foot, and when I looked down I saw a ginger-white-and-black-patched cat rubbing her face against my jeans. 'Well, hello there,' I said. The cat looked a lot like the one I'd seen at the farm gate that afternoon – both in colour and shape.

She gave a flick of her tail and padded away over to the barn before I could stroke her. But at least she'd thought I was good enough to come over to – and that was a big step up for me and cats. I grinned and snapped a picture that I planned to send to Omar when I had a spare moment. I hadn't had time to keep in contact with *anyone* since I'd arrived.

My phone bleeped. The memory was full!

I ran back up to my room, downloaded everything and added the pictures and videos to the Paw House website and YouTube channel.

By the time I'd done it and came outside again, people had moved on to dessert.

'See what Rusty thinks of this banana ice cream,' Izzy said to me, and I pressed record on my phone.

Izzy held her ice-cream cone out to the little piglet and Rusty had her first lick. A look of pure bliss crossed her face.

Steenie laughed. 'That little piglet's such a star!' And everyone agreed.

As the night drew in it grew chilly, and people moved into the house. I took Rusty over to the barn so she could sleep with Peaches and Custard.

'It's been a very busy day for you, little piglet,' I told her. I gave Custard a stroke. 'And you too,' I said, giving the calf a kiss on her soft furry brow.

In no time at all Rusty was fast asleep and I headed back to the house. There was someone over by the front door and for the briefest of seconds I worried that it might be the man who'd left Cullie come to take him back.

But it was Kenny, from the computer shop, dropping round the leaflets about the open day.

'They're perfect,' I said gratefully, as I beckoned him inside. I hid the printed T-shirts and bandanas in the shoe cupboard.

Kenny was a bit hesitant when he saw there were so many people at the house already. But Darcy, who'd been sitting behind the sofa in the corner of the room before he arrived, came over to him wagging her tail and he gave her a stroke.

'Hello, beautiful,' he said, and then he laughed with delight when he spotted Dolores and Aurora wearing their chicken outfits huddled together on the freshly washed tartan blanket that Rusty had arrived in.

Kenny knelt down beside the two chickens and I told him how much they'd enjoyed their cake crumbs. Darcy rested her chin on Kenny's shoulder and looked at the chickens too.

'My mam used to keep chickens when we were kids,' Kenny said, as Dolores stood up and started scratching at the tartan blanket with her feet. 'I can remember reading stories to them from my library books when I was still a tiny tot. I thought they understood every word! Mam's in the old people's home up the road now, but I bet she'd love to meet these two. She'd be tickled pink to see hens wearing clothes!'

'Your mother would be more than welcome anytime,' Aunt Helen said, smiling, as Kenny took out his phone to video the two chickens so his mum could see them when he visited her the next day.

‘Why don’t the old people’s home come on a trip to the open day?’ I said. ‘We’ll have plenty of food.’

‘More than enough,’ Tania grinned. ‘Plus I’m still getting messages from people wanting to bring more dishes!’

Tania had linked the Paw House website to her own successful food blog already. It was read by people all over the world who wanted to try new delicious plant-based recipes. Tania even wrote recipes for the Scottish national press.

‘If it’s popular, we could maybe make it a regular one-day-a-week pop-up sort of thing, and turn one of the sheds into a little rustic restaurant,’ she said.

‘There’s certainly room for a cafe here,’ Aunt Helen said.

I nodded. It was a great idea. The sheds weren’t being used for anything yet and were crying out for a new venture.

‘Bloggers like me are always looking for places to test out our recipes, and this would be an amazing location for photographs,’ Tania told us.

‘Plus you’d always have a very willing “helper” in little Rusty,’ laughed Izzy.

‘The old people’s home does like to take the old folks out on outings in the minibus and this could be the perfect place for them to come,’ Kenny said thoughtfully. ‘And they always stop for tea and cakes.’

Tania smiled. ‘My speciality!’

Kenny was still videoing Dolores and Aurora when something unexpected began to happen.

Dolores grasped hold of a strand of the jumper yarn with her beak and began to pull it as if it were a worm, although I doubt if she'd ever even seen a real worm in her life. Aunt Helen said chickens like Dolores and Aurora were often kept indoors in cages their whole lives. Dolores kept on pulling, just seeing how far the thread would go.

Kenny kept on videoing as we all watched in amazement.

I kept thinking this *had* to be added to the Paw House YouTube channel. Dolores was a star!

When Dolores had finally had enough, and her tabard was a lot shorter than it had started off, she let go of the strand of wool, looked straight at Kenny, gave a cluck and sat down.

'That's a wrap,' I said, and everyone laughed.

Darcy had taken a real liking to Kenny and never left his side.

'You liked him, Darcy, didn't you?' I said to the Staffie, when Kenny left.

Darcy looked up at me with her brown eyes and wagged her tail.

I straightened up and looked at Izzy. 'You know if we're going to have lots and lots of people at the open day and want to raise as much money as we can then maybe we should have some stalls too.'

'Like at the Highland Games,' Izzy said, nodding.

'And music,' Steenie said. 'I know some people.'

'My mum's in a folk band. They might come if I asked her,' Irene said.

'And there should be dancing . . .' Mrs Enders said. 'I used to do a mean Highland fling. Bet I still could do it with a little practice.'

'Entertainment.'

'A raffle . . .'

Aunt Helen looked from one of them to the other. The open day was turning into a major event.

'Sometimes I have to pinch myself to believe this is all really happening!' she said with a huge smile on her face.

No one got to bed until very late because we all kept on coming up with different ideas. When everyone, besides Aunt Helen and me, had finally left for the night, Violet stood by the door of the dogs' room where she was supposed to sleep and looked meaningfully at me. She seemed to be saying very clearly that she wanted to sleep upstairs with me, Cullie and the chickens tonight.

'Is it OK?' I asked Aunt Helen.

'Fine with me, if you want to,' she said, picking up Cullie to carry him up the stairs.

I did want to. 'Come on, Violet,' I said.

Violet and Cullie snuggled up together on the rug that I was planning to measure up in the morning and use on the float. Aurora and Dolores were in a box with a cosy blanket and the remnants of my old jumper.

Only, sometime during the night, Cullie and Violet ended up in bed with me and so did Aurora and Dolores. The chickens were perched on the wooden bedstead. Violet was at the end of the bed and Cullie's little face was the first thing I saw when I woke up in the morning, his head resting on my pillow.

Chapter 16

While Aunt Helen was giving the dogs their breakfast, I measured the rug Violet and Cullie had slept part of the night on. As I'd thought, it would fit perfectly on the floor of the float. I ate my toast and tayberry jam, and then went back out to the big shed, taking Cullie, Violet, Aurora and Dolores with me while Aunt Helen took the rest of the dogs for a walk.

At first Aurora and Dolores just sat where I put them down, but after a short while they started to explore, making little noises as if they were chatting to each other and pecking at anything that looked interesting.

But when the field mouse poked its head out of its hole they came running back to me, squawking. Their noise must have scared the mouse because it disappeared back into its hole, and Dolores and Aurora were soon back to pecking at tasty bits.

I didn't stop Cullie and Violet when they wandered off out of the shed in the direction of the barn where Rusty was. They couldn't come to any harm here, and there was still a lot to get done before the parade.

My plan was to complete the loch monster by painting it in lots of bright colours. Then once it had been varnished and was completely dry I'd cut a big hole in it and place Miss Lily's chair inside the hole – with a cushion or pillow to make her higher if need be.

To people standing on the street who saw the float go past during the parade it would look like Miss Lily was hitching a lift on the Friendly Ness's back as it swam through the water. I spent all morning working on it although the shed was baking, even with the doors wide open. Sensible Aurora and Dolores found a shady spot underneath the horse cart and went to sleep.

Aunt Helen brought me out a sandwich for lunch when I forgot to go inside for it. Mackenzie came with her.

'That's looking really amazing, Mishka,' she said, as Mackenzie lay down next to me.

'Thanks.'

The Friendly Ness had turned out really well and it looked so cheerful and bright. I'd decided to make each leg a different colour. One was orange, another pink, the third blue and the last one bright yellow. The body and head were a vivid turquoise with round splodges of vibrant paint dotted about.

As soon as I'd finished the sandwich I started working on a banner with the slogan 'The Paw House: Give a Dog a Home', and in smaller writing: 'Paws and Friends – All Animals Welcome'.

The banner was going to arch across the back of the float and I'd make another one for the front. I didn't want to attach it until just before the parade though, as the banner was quite flimsy.

'Mishka!' Aunt Helen's voice shouted suddenly. 'Mishka – come quickly!'

I dropped my paintbrush and ran out of the shed and over to Aunt Helen who was waving wildly at me with both hands from beside the duck pond.

'Phone!' she shouted, as I got closer and realized she was waving in excitement, not fright.

I pulled my phone from my pocket as I ran.

Just as well I did, because I wouldn't have wanted to have missed videoing Rusty and Cullie playing together in the duck pond and Violet watching, with her paws cooling in the water, from the side.

'Pigs are great swimmers,' Aunt Helen said, as Rusty swam around with Cullie paddling after her. 'In the wild they sometimes swim for miles.'

Cullie came out of the pond and shook himself next to me, spraying water everywhere. I didn't mind at all. Anything to cool off! Rusty came out of the water too and smiled up at me, but she didn't shake like Cullie had done.

When the puppy and piglet left the pond the ducks noisily swam back into the middle. It sounded quite a lot like the ducks were congratulating each other for frightening the intruders off!

I headed back to the hot shed. If it got too hot, I supposed I could always take a dip in the pond too!

I left Dolores and Aurora in their shady spot under the horse cart when we took the dogs for a walk in the afternoon. Izzy stayed behind with Cullie, Violet and Miss Lily. Rusty was fast asleep with Custard and Peaches in the barn.

'How've Gertie and Shadow been?' I asked Aunt Helen as we headed towards their paddock. I felt bad for not seeing them yet today, but I'd been so busy and there'd be plenty of time once the parade was over.

Aunt Helen smiled. 'I'd say they've made themselves at home.'

Shadow ran over to the gate as we got closer, with Gertie trotting along behind him.

Aunt Helen had an apple for them in her pocket. I loved watching them crunching on it. Gertie got apple juice all over her muzzle and licked it off with her long pink tongue.

We headed to the river where all the dogs got to cool off and even Aunt Helen and I had a paddle. I was tempted to have a swim too, alongside the dogs, but just managed to resist. My mum would have gone bananas if she'd seen me. I could almost hear her screaming: *Do you know how many germs there are in there? And you're swimming with DOGS!*

When we got back I completed the varnishing and then stepped back to admire the float. It had turned out even better than I'd hoped.

'Looks brilliant,' Izzy said from behind me, and I could tell by the way she said the words that she really meant it.

The float was now ready, apart from Miss Lily's chair, the rug from my room and the slogan banner. We had tons of leaflets to give out and Irene had dropped off some orange collection buckets for us to use on the day. The buckets were orange and had yellow lids with slits in them for the money to go in. 'Please give generously to Lochmarron's First Highland Games' was printed on the lids. Izzy had stuck an open day leaflet to the side of each of the buckets while we'd been walking the dogs.

Dolores and Aurora were still sitting under the horse cart and blinked at us when we looked at them.

'Should we take them back inside for the night?' I asked Izzy.

They looked so settled where they were that it seemed a bit mean to disturb them.

'They'll be OK so long as we shut the shed door. I wouldn't like a fox – or even a *faux*! – to get them,' Izzy said. She gave me a nudge and I grinned back.

The leather-jacket fiasco seemed like a very long time ago now.

While I soaked the varnish brushes, Izzy went to get Dolores and Aurora some corn for their dinner.

'Do you think they'll be ready to join the other chickens soon?' I asked her when she returned.

'Maybe,' Izzy said. 'But there's no rush. They seem happy as they are.'

I nodded and we headed over to the house for our own dinner. I was so glad Dolores and Aurora were safe now.

It felt a bit empty with only Cullie and Violet in my room with me at bedtime, and I stared down at the empty chicken box before falling into a deep sleep almost immediately.

It was very late when something disturbed the dogs downstairs and they all started barking. The barking was closely followed by the sound of tiny trotters on the stairs. The next thing I knew Rusty had pushed open my bedroom door with her snout and was squealing and squealing beside my bed.

'Ssssh, Rusty,' I told her, still half asleep. But Rusty didn't ssssh, she squealed even more and it became impossible to ignore her. Maybe something was wrong with one of the other animals? Since being here I'd learnt so much about animal friendship that it didn't seem hard to imagine she was coming to let me know something was wrong.

I jumped out of bed and ran out of my room, almost bumping into Aunt Helen.

'What is it?' I said.

'I don't know!' Aunt Helen cried. 'But I saw a light. Someone's out there.'

We ran outside with the dogs running beside us, still barking, and one little piglet squealing.

From the barn there came the most horrendous, bellowing scream I'd ever heard.

'Peaches!' Aunt Helen cried, and we ran over to the barn to see what was wrong.

We saw immediately that Custard wasn't there.

'Someone's taken Custard!' Aunt Helen shouted over the sound of Peaches' distraught bellowing, and it felt like time suddenly froze because the news was so awful. 'The gate is closed; she didn't wander out by mistake!'

'She's not old enough to be away from her mum yet,' I said, feeling sick.

Custard only drank milk from her mum. She couldn't survive without it.

'She's so vulnerable,' Aunt Helen said, fighting back tears.

'But why would anyone take her?' It seemed so cruel and pointless.

'I didn't hear a van, did you?' Aunt Helen said and I shook my head. 'Whoever it was, they must be on foot.' She released the gate to Peaches' stall. 'She'll be able to find her daughter far quicker than we can. Cattle hearing is better than humans' and she has near panoramic vision as well as an incredible sense of smell.'

Peaches stopped bellowing as she sniffed the air outside the barn and then she started again even louder.

'Is she calling to Custard?' I asked Aunt Helen.

'I think so.'

Peaches headed off down the path. The fence to Gertie and Shadow's paddock had been opened too, although I could see them safe over by the tree – thank goodness.

Peaches headed across the grass. Her fast walk turned to a trot and then a run. She was heading towards the river where we took the dogs walking. It was very deep in places.

'Highland cows are good swimmers,' Aunt Helen said, as we ran. 'But Custard's so young.'

A disoriented calf could easily slip, I thought in a panic as I ran after Peaches, but then I told my brain to shut up. I couldn't let myself think like that. We needed to find Custard. I couldn't get the image of her, just after she was born, standing on her unsteady calf legs next to her mum out of my head.

Peaches gave another of her huge bellows and stopped. There was a reply, a very faint and almost too hard to hear reply, but it was definitely something. Peaches headed on and as we hurried after her the sounds of a frightened baby calf became clearer.

'There she is!' Aunt Helen said, pointing to the left of us.

Custard had been left tied to a tree not far from the river. She was trembling with fear, but very glad to see her mum.

Peaches ran to her daughter and licked her over and over and made soft soothing noises. Custard kept making noises too; it was almost as if she was telling her mum what had happened.

'Do you think more animals were taken?' I asked, suddenly frightened again. Now Aunt Helen looked really worried.

'Oh, Mishka –'

I raced back to the sanctuary as fast as I could leaving Aunt Helen to bring Custard and Peaches home.

In the barn Woolly and Jock blinked at me sleepily. Gertie and Shadow had decided to sleep outside in the paddock because it was so warm. The chickens and noisy cockerel were undisturbed.

I headed over to the float shed to check on Dolores and Aurora. But as soon as I pulled open the door I gasped in horror. My friendly loch monster had been torn off the horse cart, pulled apart and spray-painted across its neck and belly in blood-red paint. It looked like it had been murdered!

Aunt Helen gasped in disbelief, as she came running in behind me. 'Why would someone do this?'

All I could think about was Dolores and Aurora. They'd been under the horse cart. Were they OK?

I grabbed Aunt Helen's torch and knelt down among the papier-mâché mess. Two small tabard-wearing chickens blinked back at me, and in between them was a tortoise. As soon as Dolores and Aurora saw me they came running, squawking. The tortoise came after them, not as fast as the chickens, but still pretty fast for a tortoise that had been alive during the Second World War.

'Hello, Tommy,' I said. 'Nice to meet you at last.'

I breathed a sigh of relief as I cuddled the chickens to me and gave Tommy a stroke until he had enough of that and went back under the horse cart.

'All your hard work. Your beautiful float,' Aunt Helen said, horrified.

'It's OK,' I told her. Dolores, Aurora and Tommy were unhurt and they were much more important than a papier-mâché sculpture. I pulled my phone from my pocket and took photos and then a video of the wreckage. This was going on the internet. I wanted as many people as possible to know what had happened.

'Do you think it was Cyrus and his friends?' I asked Aunt Helen.

But Aunt Helen shook her head. 'They're good boys really. *Surely* it couldn't have been them.' I thought Aunt Helen was too trusting. Cyrus and his friends were bad news.

We headed back to the main house with me carrying Dolores and Aurora and Aunt Helen bringing Tommy.

She phoned the police from the kitchen and was told someone would be there as soon as possible.

'They said not to touch anything until they come,' Aunt Helen said, when the call was over.

I nodded. We'd both seen enough crime dramas on TV to know not to tamper with possible evidence.

We gave Tommy some lettuce to snack on and the chickens a few cornflakes.

I tried not to yawn as I listened to Dolores and Aurora making little crunching sounds as they pecked at the cornflakes but I couldn't help myself.

'Why don't you go to bed, Mishka?' Aunt Helen said. 'You must be exhausted. I'll deal with the police. You take Dolores and Aurora upstairs with you.' I was going to say no, but Aunt Helen continued gently, 'Go on, Mishka. There's nothing more you can do. Custard's home safe and sound and none of the other animals were injured. But I'm so sorry about all your hard work being ruined. I suppose the parade's off after all.'

I totally agreed with her that the most important thing was that none of the animals had been seriously injured by the vandals. But I didn't agree at all about us withdrawing from the parade.

'If we're not part of the parade, it'll mean whoever did this has won,' I said. 'And I'm not going to let them win!'

Chapter 17

Aunt Helen was already making breakfast in the kitchen when I came downstairs early the next morning with Dolores and Aurora.

'I told Constable Campbell what happened last night and he took lots of photos as evidence,' she told me.

'Would kidnapping Custard count as cattle rustling?' I asked her, setting the chickens on the floor and sitting down at the table. 'That's a crime, right?'

Aunt Helen shook her head. 'I asked Constable Campbell that and he said yes and no. "Cattle rustling is a crime," he said, "but moving a calf half a mile away and leaving it there might be considered more of a prank." '

'Custard could have died!' I said.

'I know,' said Aunt Helen sadly. 'Whoever took Custard and vandalized your float must really hate animals – or maybe they hate how kind we are to them.'

I pulled out my phone. I'd put the photos and video of the damage on the internet last night and now I showed Aunt Helen the hundreds and hundreds of people who'd been outraged and left comments of support for the Paw House. 'More good people than bad.'

She smiled. 'I know,' she said. 'It was just such a shock. A violation.'

When Steenie and Izzy arrived and heard what had happened they were horrified.

'You should have called me,' Steenie told Aunt Helen. He was wearing a blue kilt and long socks, all ready for the Games. 'I'd have come straight away.'

'And me!' said Izzy.

'It was very late,' Aunt Helen told them tiredly. 'Constable Campbell came out – there was nothing you could have done.'

But Steenie and Izzy didn't look like they agreed. We all headed over to the shed so they could see the wrecked float.

Izzy and Steenie stared down at the poor papier-mâché monster. One of its short stubby legs was completely broken off from the chicken wire frame and lay like a hollow Easter egg on the floor.

But as I looked at its other three brightly painted stubby legs and squashed body I suddenly saw how I could turn our poor Friendly Ness into something else! Something even better.

'Maybe I should phone Irene and say we won't be taking part in the parade after all,' Aunt Helen said, putting her hand on my shoulder.

'No!' I said, and it came out as a shout. 'I can fix it. You know the tartan blanket Rusty was wrapped in when we first met her?'

'Yes.'

'Do you mind if I chop it up?'

'Not at all. What are you thinking, Mishka?'

'You'll see,' I called over my shoulder as I ran back to the house to fetch the blanket while the three of them went to check on the rest of the animals.

When I came back out Aunt Helen was just going inside with Rusty and a black-and-tan dog I recognized immediately as Homer.

'Look who I found fast asleep next to Rusty in Peaches and Custard's stall,' Aunt Helen said.

Homer was holding his right front paw off the ground as if it were hurt. I followed them into the kitchen.

'Now let me take a look at that paw,' Aunt Helen said to Homer.

The dog docilely let Aunt Helen look at his paw but he must have been in pain because he gave a whimper every now and again and licked her hand.

Rusty stayed close to her new friend while Aunt Helen cleaned and bandaged the wound.

'Yes, you have been very good and very brave,' Aunt Helen told Homer when she was done. 'And I'm sure you'll be glad to know it's now breakfast time.'

Rusty jumped up and gave a squee. It was almost as if she'd heard the word 'breakfast' and thought she'd like some too.

Homer was really hungry and gulped his food down in two seconds flat. Rusty had melon and some of the leftover food from yesterday as her pre-breakfast breakfast because she'd have her proper one with Peaches and Custard later.

After she'd finished her food Rusty nuzzled her head into me and I gave her a gentle scratch. She wriggled around so I could be sure to scratch under her chin and along her back as well. If she hadn't come in through the cat flap and alerted us last night we wouldn't have known that Custard had been taken.

'Thank you, little pig,' I said, and then I headed back out to the shed with the red tartan blanket. Now to get busy with scissors and glue.

It didn't take long to put my grand plan into action: transforming the poor Friendly Ness from a loch monster into one giant paw! I created four different-coloured toes and a turquoise paw pad. This was going on the front of the cart. I quickly painted two new banners, as the orginals had been destroyed by the vandals, to put on the back and sides – along with some smaller paw prints that I cut out of the tartan blanket. And Lily, in her chair, and Blue, not in a chair, would go in the middle – to show the range of dog sizes we had – all looking for loving homes.

'Very effective,' Steenie said, when he came to see how I was getting on a little while later.

'And luckily very quick,' I said. It was almost time to go!

We headed back to the house with Steenie pulling and me pushing the decorated cart.

'Not too heavy at all!' Steenie said, as we left the cart and went inside.

'I have a surprise for you,' I said, as I took the Paw House T-shirts from their hiding place in the shoe cupboard and gave them out.

'It's XXXL,' I told Steenie.

Even so the vest T-shirt was a bit tight and he looked like he was bursting out of it.

'Talk about the Incredible Hulk.' Izzy laughed, and Steenie did too.

I put the bandanas that Kenny had printed paw prints on round the necks of the four dogs that were taking part in the parade with us. Miss Lily wasn't keen on me putting hers on her. But luckily once it was on she just gave me a lofty glare and didn't try to take it off.

'Now we look like a team,' I said, as I pulled my own Paw House T-shirt over my head.

Izzy helped me to carry down the rug from my room and put it on the painted floor of the old wooden horse cart. Then we lifted the mustard yellow chair, with Miss Lily still in it, on to the cart. She growled and bared her teeth at us but she didn't move a centimetre – just as I'd hoped.

Blue didn't get on the float yet, but Miss Lily would be sitting in her chair all the way to the parade start.

We talked about it and although Aurora and Dolores probably would have stayed on the float it didn't seem fair to put them on it after last night's ordeal.

'If people want to see them they can come to the open day,' Aunt Helen said.

Mrs Enders and some of Steenie's friends, as well as Irene and her husband, Ray, came to look after the animals while we were away. I still thought Cyrus, Donut and Jay were the culprits of last night's vandalism and Izzy agreed with me. Our new security guards were given strict instructions to phone the police and Aunt Helen immediately if there was anyone suspicious lurking about or anything seemed wrong.

'I'd like to see anyone try to get past us!' Mrs Enders said, and she managed to look very fierce, despite having lots of ribbons in her hair.

By the time we left, the doors leading from the stalls in the barn to the green paddock outside were all open, but there were people sitting out in the sunshine watching the animals to make sure they were safe. Shadow and Gertie usually headed outside as soon as they'd had their breakfast, but Peaches and Custard came in and out quite a lot during the day and Jock and Woolly didn't like to rush. At the Paw House the animals could come and go as they liked.

Steenie pulled the float and I tried to help him by pushing it, but I don't think I was much help really. Aunt Helen had Blue and Mackenzie with her. Izzy had Darcy. Violet and Cullie were staying behind and no doubt being made a fuss of by Irene and Ray.

The other floats were already lined up when we arrived. For a small place I thought it was a really good turn-out. There were pirate floats and beauty queens and cartoon character floats – and plenty more besides. The Chieftain of the Games' float was at the front behind the Lochmarron Junior High School piping band that was going to lead the procession.

As well as the floats there were clowns and people on stilts and Highland dancers in traditional costumes. We took our place at the back.

'That's it, Blue. Good dog. Sit. Stay.' Aunt Helen said, as she encouraged Blue on to the float. Blue stayed in his place in front of Miss Lily's chair, despite the fierce little growls that came from her.

'Excuse me,' a man said to Aunt Helen. 'Could I have a word with you about my dog? I've been leaving him at home when I'm at work but now I've had a letter of complaint about his barking.'

I put my thumbs up to Izzy as Aunt Helen told him about the Paw House's new doggie day-care that was just about to open. Ongoing paying guests would be perfect!

'This is it!' Steenie said, as a shrill whistle blew.

The atmosphere was buzzing with excitement as we set off.

Darcy was fine until the bagpipes and drums started playing. But then she started shaking and making little whimpering sounds.

Aunt Helen and Mackenzie were behind us, still talking to the man with the barking dog.

'It's all right, Darcy,' Izzy soothed her. 'There's nothing to be frightened of.'

But Darcy didn't stop and it was too late to take her back to the Paw House. She'd have to carry on.

Lots of people cheered as our float went by. Steenie was well known in the area and he had lots of friends who were egging him on loudly.

'Go on, Steenie – you can do it!'

'It's like pulling a pram!'

But among all the excitement something was wrong. Ahead of us I could see the three bullies. Cyrus had grabbed Izzy's collection bucket and was trying to pull it away from her. Izzy was pulling the other way but she wasn't really a match for Cyrus. And poor Darcy was cowering away, terrified.

'Leave her alone!' I yelled. But Cyrus didn't stop and now Donut and Jay started to join in too. They were shoving at Izzy. But she wouldn't give them her bucket. The money in it was for the Games and the Paw House and other local charities, not them.

I looked at Blue. He was sitting still, but I couldn't help thinking he looked a bit bored. I knew the only danger from Blue was excessive slobber and he'd be far more likely to give a lick than a bite . . . but the bullies didn't know that. I had an idea.

'Blue,' I called. 'Go find Izzy. Go find her!' And I pointed to where she was. Blue was off the float in one Great Dane bound and lolloping through a troop of Highland dancers, who all swiftly moved out of his way, as he headed towards Izzy.

I pulled out my phone and started filming as I ran after Blue.

He soon reached the bullies and they were backing away – fast – but they were cornered by the wall behind them. Izzy still had hold of her charity bucket but her jacket was torn and her hair was messy.

Blue sat down beside Izzy.

Izzy pointed at Cyrus and then looked at the dog. 'Kisses, Blue!'

Blue knew exactly what he was supposed to do and immediately went over to the boys, stood on his hind legs so he was the same height as Cyrus and started licking his face while Cyrus desperately tried to get away. He was no match for Blue.

'No, no! Leave me alone! Call your dog off!' Cyrus begged, as he held his arms over his head. 'Call it off!'

I filmed it all on my phone. Every last moment.

'This'll look good on the internet,' I told Cyrus, Donut and Jay. 'And that's where it's going to end up if you three bother us again.'

They swore at me a bit, but then they slunk off.

Izzy grinned at me and then we high-fived. 'Not bad,' she said. 'Not bad at all.'

The bagpipes and drums started playing 'Scotland the Brave'. Poor Darcy was shaking and looking utterly miserable.

'I think it's because the music's so loud,' Izzy said. 'Dogs' hearing is very sensitive.'

'It's OK, Darcy,' I said, trying to soothe her. I wished we hadn't brought her. I hated seeing her so distressed.

Then a familiar voice said, 'I could take her back to the sanctuary if you like.' It was Kenny from the computer shop.

'Oh, yes please,' Izzy and I said.

'If she'll come with me,' Kenny added, but Darcy looked up at him and wagged her tail.

I was pretty sure Darcy was thinking, 'Thank goodness that's over!' as the two of them walked away.

'You two,' Steenie yelled. 'Can we get back to work now?'

I ran back to the float with Blue and the dog jumped on board.

'Sorry. Emergency,' I told Steenie.

I went back to collecting money and giving out leaflets about the open day tomorrow.

With a groan Steenie was off again. I could see a policeman talking to the bullies. They were pointing at Izzy and me and Blue, who was now lying down innocently on the float with his head in his paws. I hoped we weren't going to be in trouble. He'd only been licking Cyrus, after all.

'Excuse me,' an elderly woman said. 'That dog in the chair . . .'

'She's called Miss Lily. Yes?'

'Well, I have to say, she looks so like my Flora. When did you rescue her exactly?'

'A few months ago, I think. You'd be better asking . . .' I pointed in Aunt Helen's direction, but the woman continued.

'I was on the way to visit my daughter on the coast and stopped at a garage and that's when she somehow got out of the car. One moment she was there and the next she was gone. I've been worrying ever since. She's such a tiny little thing! Oh – I'm just so *sure* that's her!'

I gave the woman one of the leaflets. 'Why don't you come to the Paw House Open Day?' I said. I really needed to catch up with the float – which was now way ahead of me. 'I have to go – but see you tomorrow!'

I raced after the float, collecting money and giving out leaflets to anyone who would take them as I ran.

Finally the parade ended at the recreation ground where there were stalls selling souvenirs and ice creams, tartans, and jams, as well as a mini fun fair with a bouncy castle, children's train ride and a carousel. The Chieftain of the Games, an elderly man wearing a kilt, stood on the stage holding a silver-topped shepherd's crook.

'Every year someone different will be chosen to be the Chieftain, but this first year it's Dr Blythe. He's treated the sick of Lochmarron for the last fifty years,' Steenie told me. 'Good man.'

I nodded as Blue looked up at me and I stroked him. He'd jumped off the float as soon as it had stopped but Miss Lily was still in her armchair and had no intention of moving. Mackenzie was with Aunt Helen as usual.

Dr Blythe held up a long sword and a round shield.

'The champion of the Games will be awarded those at the end of the day,' Aunt Helen told me, as the Chieftain hit the shield with the sword four times and declared the Games open.

Steenie went to join the other four heavy athletes that were competing. They all had muscles on top of muscles like Steenie and were wearing different coloured kilts. I was glad he was wearing his vest advertising the Paw House. Aunt Helen and the dogs stayed with the float while Izzy and I headed over to the ice cream stall.

'Have you got any non-dairy ice creams?' Izzy asked the seller.

'Yep – lots! And fruit sorbets,' he told her.

We bought five coconut milk ice cream cones and headed back to Aunt Helen with them. As soon as Mackenzie and Blue saw us – or maybe it was the ice creams – they started wagging their tails.

I broke the bottom of my cone off and scooped some ice cream in it. We hadn't got Miss Lily a cone of her own because she was such a little dog.

'Here, Miss Lily, what's this?' I said, as I held it out to her.

I wasn't sure if she'd eat it or not and was delighted when her little tongue came out and she started licking it.

'That's it,' I said. 'That's it, Miss Lily. Here, have some more.' I scooped a bit more into the mini cone.

'Dairy can upset dogs tummies,' Aunt Helen told me, as Mackenzie crunched up his cone, 'but coconut milk's usually fine.'

Izzy helped Blue to eat his ice cream, not that he needed it! One great swipe of his huge tongue and it was just about gone and he looked at Izzy's cone hopefully.

That look reminded me of a little piglet.

'Rusty would love this ice cream,' I said, thinking back to how much she'd liked the banana one at the BBQ.

'Hey there!' a familiar voice said, and when I looked round I saw that Irene was making her way over.

'Is everything all right?' Aunt Helen asked.

'Completely fine,' Irene said. 'More than fine in fact!' She gave a sort of half-wink to Izzy.

'I think I might go home now you're here,' Aunt Helen said distractedly. 'I can take Mackenzie and Blue with me. You can stay here and watch the Games with Izzy, Mishka.'

'No!' Irene blurted out.

Aunt Helen's brow furrowed.

'You have to stay,' Irene said firmly.

'Why?' Aunt Helen asked.

Irene sighed. 'They're getting a surprise ready for you back at the Paw House,' she said. 'I'll need your help in a bit, Izzy.'

'A surprise? But everyone's done so much already!' Aunt Helen said.

'Just let them do this tiny bit more,' Irene said with a twinkle in her eye. 'Come on now. Let's go and watch the Highland dancing.'

She took Aunt Helen's arm and almost dragged her away. Mackenzie headed after them.

Blue sniffed at the grass checking for any dropped ice cream.

'I'll watch Miss Lily on the float,' Izzy said. 'You don't want to miss the *Gillie Callum*, Mishka.'

I ran after Aunt Helen and Irene, but I couldn't help wondering what the surprise might be. After I'd watched an intricate sword dance over two crossed swords I headed back to Izzy to find out just what was going on.

'Oh good! You can watch the dogs,' Izzy shouted, before I'd even reached her. 'I didn't want to miss the wellie throwing contest.'

'Wait!' I called after her, as she ran off but she didn't stop. Blue looked up at me and then went running after her.

I climbed onto the float to check on our fierce little chihuahua. Miss Lily was staring at the back of the mustard armchair.

I wished I could stroke the lonely dog.

'Yes!' I heard Izzy shout from across the field and I watched as the wellie she'd chosen from the pile of old wellington boots on the side went flying through the air – and Blue went chasing after it.

When the time came for Steenie to toss the caber I stared down at the tapered telegraph pole lying on the grass and shook my head. It was huge.

'Almost six meters,' Steenie told me, 'And eighty kilos.'

It weighed more than me! Why would anyone want to throw it?

'Good luck,' I said, as he headed over to the line-up.

With a grunt Steenie lifted the heavy caber, ran a few steps and threw it up in the air. Then the other four athletes each took turns to do the same. But it was Steenie's throw that measured the furthest because of the way it had landed – away from him.

'I can't believe it!' Steenie grinned, when he was announced the winner. He looked very happy indeed.

The next event for the heavy athletes was carrying the smithy stone that I knew Steenie had been practising for.

'See if you can lift it,' he grinned at me, and I grabbed hold of the metal handle on the top of the stone and heaved. The 113 kilo stone didn't move so much as a millimetre.

'Impossible,' I gasped.

Luckily it wasn't impossible for Steenie.

'Go Steenie, go!' I yelled.

He wasn't so much walking as waddling with it, but he waddled further than the other four when it was their turn – an unbeatable win. 'Yeah, Steenie!'

Behind me I heard Mackenzie barking and saw that Aunt Helen was standing on the float and clapping and cheering too.

Steenie grinned and put his thumbs up to her.

He didn't end up winning the hammer throw but it didn't matter – he was still as pleased as could be with his performance.

'Not bad for my first time in the Games! I could get used to this!' he said.

The last event of the day was a giant tug of war that everyone was invited to take part in. Nearly everyone did, including Aunt Helen and me. On the other team an enthusiastic elderly American man was pulling for all he was worth and going red in the face from the effort. I was *sure* he was the man who'd sat next to me on the train.

'For the ancestors!' he shouted, having a whale of a time.

We couldn't stop cheering when Steenie was named Champion of the Games and given the shield and the sword by the Chieftain.

'I'm honoured to give the Champion's sword and shield to a man I've known ever since he was a wee bairn. In fact I delivered him!' Dr Blythe said, and people cheered as Steenie took the sword and shield and held them up high over his head.

The Chieftain said everyone was welcome to stay for the ceilidh party and BBQ, and to our delight he reminded everyone that tomorrow there was an open day at the Paw House: 'Our local animal sanctuary.'

Aunt Helen squeezed my hand and I grinned.

After the ceremony, Steenie headed over to us with the four other heavy athletes.

'The lads have offered to help with the float,' he said. 'Although we'll be coming straight back for the ceilidh afterwards!'

Mackenzie wagged his tail as the athletes each gave him a stroke and then he jumped up onto the float and sat at the front of it like a ship's figurehead on the journey home.

Chapter 18

'Would you look at all this! I've never met such a lot of busy bees,' Mrs Enders said, with a big smile on her face when we got back. She was sitting on a garden lounger in the sunshine with Rusty. Homer was lying next to them. When we'd left for the parade the garden lounger had been its plain, greyish white self, but now it was covered in a big multicoloured knitted blanket and looked very cosy indeed.

'What do you mean?' Aunt Helen asked her, and Mrs Enders got up to show us.

'This way!'

Something wonderful had happened to the Paw House. It was as if a rainbow had dropped down on to it while we'd been at the parade.

'What's happened?' Aunt Helen said delightedly, as she looked around. There were hundreds of knitted hearts in the tree Violet liked to sit under. The fences had bright yarn wrapped round them and the house itself had been wrapped in big knitted squares.

'We've been yarn-bombed!' I told her. I didn't know who'd arranged it. Yarn bombers aren't usually big on self-publicity. But I remembered all those wonderful people who had been disgusted by the vandalism photos I'd posted on the internet. 'The Paw House must have a lot of fans!'

'What's yarn-bombing?' asked Aunt Helen, running her hand along the line of wool across the top of the fence.

'Graffiti knitting and crocheting.' I told her. 'They did it over in Selkirk a few years ago. Called themselves the Souter Stormers. The oldest person in that group was a hundred and four years old!'

My hero the famous street artist Banksy said, 'Some people become vandals because they want to make the world a better-looking place', and the guerrilla knitters certainly did that!

'They said they just wanted to show their support,' Mrs Enders told Aunt Helen, and we both pretended not to notice when Aunt Helen brushed away a tear.

Not only had the whole place been brightened up, but more of Steenie's friends had transformed the chicken house into a true Chicken Castle complete with turrets and lots of little rope swings for the chickens to perch and swing on.

It wasn't only the chickens' home that had been transformed. 'Hoof Hotel' had a freshly painted sign at the front and 'welcome' was painted in bright colours on the ground.

'Oh my,' Aunt Helen said. 'That's lovely.'

'Looking very cheery,' Mrs Enders agreed, with Rusty trotting along beside her.

The animals' names and copies of the cartoon drawings I'd done of them for the open day leaflet were painted above their stalls, along with laminated print-outs and photographs telling the story of how each animal came to be at the sanctuary. Izzy must have helped with that bit.

One of the sheds had also been cleaned up.

'This is actually a pretty nice space,' Aunt Helen said.

'Could use it for meetings and classes,' Mrs Enders agreed. 'One of the yarn bombers said they'd be interested in hiring it for their art class.'

'Good idea!' I said. I hoped the class would start before I had to leave so I could join in.

'Did they indeed?' Aunt Helen said with a big smile on her face. She gave my arm a squeeze and I grinned at her.

We went to check on Gertie and Shadow, who were out in the paddock, their fence now wrapped in colourful yarn, and then Mrs Enders headed off back home through the orchard. I saw that some of her trees had been decorated with pom-poms and crocheted flowers too.

Kenny was waiting for us at the house with Darcy.

'Thanks, Kenny,' I said. I knew he must have been the one who'd printed out the laminated sheets and photographs.

'This printer from the shop's going spare,' he said to Aunt Helen, nodding at the one on the ground beside him.

Aunt Helen bit her bottom lip. 'You've been so generous – I should pay . . .' she started to say, but Kenny shook his head before she could finish.

'I'm only going to recycle it for spare parts if you can't take it,' he told her.

'We can!' I said, as Darcy looked up at Kenny and he gave her furry head a stroke.

'Thanks for bringing Darcy home,' Aunt Helen said. 'The Highland Games parade was a bit traumatic for her.'

'Bit traumatic for me too.' Kenny smiled. 'Darcy's such a lovely dog. Is she one of those that are – er – available for rehoming?'

'Yes she is,' said Aunt Helen, and she started to tell him about the procedure for adopting a rescue dog, which included a home visit. 'I'm sure yours will be fine,' she said. 'But it is one of the rules.'

I thought Aunt Helen would need to be telling those rules to Irene and Ray soon if they decided to adopt Cullie and Violet, which I was sure they were going to.

Kenny said he completely understood, and that he wouldn't want Darcy to go anywhere that wasn't approved of first. Darcy looked after him and gave a whine as he left.

'He'll be back soon,' I told her, and thought with a smile about how one day they might not have to be parted at all.

Then Izzy came in with Blue and I grabbed my phone to show her the footage of Blue and the bullies. There was a text on my phone from Mum and Dad about a Sumo wrestling match they'd been to and a surprise they had for me. The text was from yesterday but I hadn't had the time to text back.

Izzy laughed and laughed as she watched the video I'd taken. 'Blue, you're the best,' she said, and she stroked the Great Dane, who looked very pleased with himself, although not quite sure why he should be. His huge tongue came out and he licked Izzy on the face.

'Excuse me,' a soft voice said, and when I looked round I saw the elderly lady from the parade. 'I hope you don't mind, but I just have to know if the dog on your float is my sweet little Flora and I can't wait until the open day tomorrow. My name's Agnes Reagan.'

I took Agnes to the dogs' room where Miss Lily was dozing in her armchair, which she hadn't got out of even when we'd lifted it off of the float so one of Steenie's friends could bring it home on the back of his trailer.

'Hello, Flora . . .' said Agnes.

Miss Lily sat up and then stood up and started wagging her tail.

Agnes went closer to her. 'It *is* you!'

Her voice caught in her throat. And that was when Miss Lily, or Flora, leapt into Agnes's arms and licked and licked her face as if she was never going to stop.

'Flora, oh, Flora!' Agnes kept saying over and over.

Agnes sat down in the armchair and Flora curled up in her lap.

'As soon as she saw that chair she claimed it,' Aunt Helen said, coming in and seeing the two of them together. 'And woe betide anyone else – dog or human – who thought they might sit in it instead.'

'We sit in a chair just like this one at home, don't we, Flora?' Agnes said.

I had never seen the chihuahua look so happy.

'Cup of tea?' Izzy asked Agnes.

'Yes please,' Agnes said with a smile.

It was easy to see from Miss Lily's new cheery demeanour and all the photos of her that Agnes had in her handbag that this was indeed her beloved Flora.

A short while later we waved goodbye to the two of them.

'I expect it'll take a while for any of the other dogs to be brave enough to sit in Miss Lily's chair, even though she's gone,' Aunt Helen said with a laugh, as we headed back inside.

But it wasn't a dog who sat in it next, it was the vet, Sheena, and it was less than an hour later. Sheena had arrived with a card for Aunt Helen and the oldest dog that I'd ever seen. A black Labrador with blue eyes.

'This is Nicole,' Sheena said.

'She looks very old,' I said. The dog's muzzle was covered in grey and she didn't look at all steady on her feet.

'Hello, Nicole,' Aunt Helen said, and the old dog looked up at her and gave a slow wag of her tail.

'Nearly eighteen,' said Sheena. 'But not in pain, eating well. Only her owner is too ill to look after her any more and I wondered if you could?'

Nicole lay down next to Miss Lily's old chair and Sheena sat down in it. 'I've known Nicole since she was a puppy,' she said. 'Can you take her in and do you have room? I'll cover all her food and medical bills.'

'Of course we can,' Aunt Helen said. 'She'll be a calming influence on the other dogs – and little Rusty.'

A powerful aroma filled the room. I looked down at Nicole and she looked back at me guiltily. Definitely the culprit. But what's a smell or two among friends?

'It's not her fault; she's just very old,' Aunt Helen said. 'Older dogs sometimes need a special diet for their tummies. Will you take a look at Homer's paw for me while you're here, Sheena? I gave it a clean and bandaged it up this morning and it looked good to me then, but I'd be happier if you checked it too.'

'Of course,' Sheena said.

But when we looked for Homer we couldn't find him anywhere.

'I expect he's gone home,' Aunt Helen said. 'He doesn't usually stay for very long. His paw can't have been too painful.'

A moment later Izzy came bursting into the room, making us all jump. 'Have you heard?' she cried.

'It's all right, Nicole,' Sheena said, giving the old dog a stroke.

'What's wrong?' Aunt Helen asked Izzy.

We could see by her face that something bad had happened.

'Someone's broken into the Highland Games office at the library. They've stolen the collection money!'

Aunt Helen's face went pale. 'Was anyone hurt?' she asked.

Izzy shook her head.

I could hardly believe it – everyone's hard work, an amazing day – and now this!

'They'll be caught; whoever it was won't get away with it,' Sheena said. 'Everyone knows everyone around here. Someone will have seen something.'

'At least no one was hurt,' Aunt Helen said. 'Let's hope whoever it was is caught quickly.'

All we could do was let the police do their job. We still had to get ready for the open day – tomorrow!

Chapter 19

'This is it,' Aunt Helen said, looking up at the clock. It was just before ten o'clock on Sunday morning.

We were as ready as we were going to get for the open day and had all been up for hours. Izzy and I had swept the yarn-bombed pathways and mopped the floors, not to mention helping with the huge house tidy and bathroom clean. My mum would have been very impressed!

Aunt Helen wanted the people that came to the open day to be free to go where they liked. The thief who'd stolen the Games money hadn't been caught yet – and nor had the vandals that had taken Custard and wrecked the Paw House float. But we were determined that it wouldn't stop us having a wonderful day.

The card Sheena had given Aunt Helen yesterday was on the mantelpiece. It had a quote by Ernest Hemingway and a picture of a cartoon dog and a person sitting on a bench together in the sunset. Paw in hand and hand in paw. Inside was written

'The best way to find out if you can trust somebody is to trust them.'

Aunt Helen seemed to have taken the card's message to heart.

I didn't feel quite so trusting of people after the vandalism and the stolen money. But I couldn't dwell on that now. Our Open Day visitors were about to arrive.

Tania and two of her friends were outside in the sunshine, loading up the three folding decorating tables she'd brought with her to lay out the piles of food they'd brought with them.

Steenie had just finished setting up a small stage borrowed from the Highland Games and was testing the microphone with Kenny.

Aunt Helen smiled around at everyone. 'I do hope people bring their dogs with them when they come. Not to give them up, of course, but to try out the agility course and have a go at the waggiest-tail contest!'

It wasn't long before people started arriving. I spotted the American tourist and Steenie's athlete friends.

'Hey, Mackenzie!' the athletes said, and Mackenzie wagged his tail and went over to them for a stroke.

I thought there were going be a lot of strokes for all the animals here today.

Many of the visitors wanted to know where Rusty was as soon as they came in through the gate.

'We've seen her on YouTube.'

'Instagram . . .'

'Facebook . . .'

'She's so adorable.'

I'd thought maybe fifty people would come to the open day. But in no time at all the sanctuary was filled with what I thought was at least a hundred – and still more people came. It looked like all of Tania's food would be gone in no time. Some people had heard about the Paw House yesterday at the Games, but more people had heard about it via the internet and from watching Rusty on YouTube.

'I'm feeling really nervous,' Aunt Helen told me, but then she gave a laugh and shrugged. 'How silly I am! The animals don't need me to be nervous – they need me to tell their stories and help people to fall in love with them!'

She took a deep breath and stepped on to the stage, ready to speak into the microphone.

'Thank you, everyone, for joining us. Our aim for today is to share with you all just how amazing the animals we have here at the Paw House are. In fact, how amazing *all* animals are . . .' she began.

Everyone went quiet as Izzy led Rusty up the two steps of the small stage that Aunt Helen was standing on.

'This is Rusty,' Aunt Helen said, and Rusty sat down and put out her little trotter to her. 'And she loves treats, just like all animals,' Aunt Helen gave her one.

Rusty stood up and made a small circle one way and then back the other way as everyone went 'ooooh' and 'aaaah' and 'Isn't she cute?'. Rusty was such an absolute star, and even if she did nothing all day other than be her waggy-tailed friendly self I knew that would be enough.

Joyce, who'd found the little piglet at the side of the road, stood next to me in the crowd. She clapped and clapped and mopped at her eyes and took pictures of Rusty on her phone as Aunt Helen told everyone about Rusty's antics. Her husband still had a grumpy look about him but I noticed that didn't stop the American man from telling him all about his long-lost ancestors.

Next Aunt Helen introduced Mackenzie and gave him a dog treat.

Mackenzie sat down and put his paw out for a second one, which Aunt Helen gave him and then he rolled on to his back for a tummy rub as she told everyone how she'd found him injured at the side of the road and thanked Sheena for all her help.

'Even though we couldn't save all of his legs after the accident he manages just fine on three – which you'll see for yourselves if you watch him doing the agility course!'

Then it was Blue's turn and people laughed and clapped when he gave Aunt Helen a 'kiss'.

Darcy spent the whole time she was on the small stage staring at Kenny and she ran over to him as soon as Aunt Helen let go of her lead.

Irene and Ray had formally asked if they could adopt Cullie and Violet and they came out on stage with them. Irene and Ray looked a bit embarrassed being stared at. But Cullie didn't mind at all and wagged and wagged his tail while Violet watched him from behind with what I was sure was a gentle smile.

'And I'd like to say a big welcome to our newest Paw House dog, Nicole,' Aunt Helen said, pointing to Nicole who was sitting next to Sheena. 'We hope you'll be very happy here.'

'I know she will be,' said Sheena.

'Anyone would be!' shouted Mrs Enders.

'Of course we don't only have Rusty and the dogs here,' Aunt Helen said into the microphone. 'Please follow me over to the barn and the paddock to meet some of our other guests.'

All the farm animals were free to go to the paddock from the barn whenever they wanted to, thanks to the outside doors from each stall. But none of us expected they'd want to be outside with all the visitors milling around. But that was where we were wrong.

Custard, in particular, seemed to think it was her job to present her head for a stroke to just about everyone that came to see her, and Peaches was standing right next to her. It was like the animals knew this was a very important day. Or maybe they just wanted to be friends.

None of the animals at the Paw House had to do anything they didn't want to and Aunt Helen didn't ask Shadow to do anything at all, but he jumped over the fences and pushed a new giant beach ball around the field as if he'd been doing it his whole life.

'Nice foal,' a man said. 'Might make a good rider for my daughter.'

'Well, he'd have to go with his best friend the donkey,' Aunt Helen told him. 'They come as a pair.'

The man shook his head. 'I only want the foal.'

'Then I can't let him go,' Aunt Helen said, and I smiled.

'Not much of a rescue centre if you don't let the animals go!' the man said, as he brushed past me.

Aunt Helen bit her lip and I put my arm round her shoulders and gave her a squeeze.

'He's an *eejit*,' I said, and Aunt Helen laughed.

'Can I stroke the kittens?' a little girl asked us.

'What kittens?' Aunt Helen asked her.

'We don't have any kittens at the moment,' I said.

But the little girl nodded and pointed to the barn.

'Show us,' Aunt Helen said.

Inside the barn, over in a corner where no one could reach them, was a ginger-white-and-black cat with two kittens.

'Oh!' Aunt Helen said with a smile. 'I wonder when they arrived. Those kittens can only be a few days old.'

'I'd like a kitten,' the little girl said.

'We've never had one before,' said her mother.

'Why don't you come back and visit and when they're old enough you could help to look after the kittens and maybe give them a stroke too,' Aunt Helen said to the little girl, who beamed and nodded.

I watched as the mother cat licked her newborns. She was definitely the one who'd rubbed her face against me over by the paddock. The first cat that had actually liked me! I snapped a quick picture of the kittens for Omar. I had a couple of unread messages but had to get back to the animals. I could give everyone an update after today!

Gertie's previous owner turned up a little while later with his daughter, bringing apples for Gertie and Shadow.

'You look positively blooming, old girl,' he told the donkey, as he kissed her on her grey muzzle. 'This place obviously agrees with you!' He grinned with the few remaining teeth he had left in his mouth, his eyes shining.

'You're welcome to come and see her and Shadow any time you like,' Aunt Helen said.

'And we always need more volunteers,' I added. I'd been trying to persuade as many people as I could to help even if it was only for an hour or so each week. The local school wanted to help grow some food for the animals in the garden. And a few other brave souls, including Kenny, had agreed to help with mucking out.

'Might just do that,' the old man said. 'I need something to occupy me now Shadow and Gertie are gone. And this place – this place has got a feel of home about it.'

Gertie nuzzled her muzzle against him.

A woman came over to us. 'I hope you don't mind but I was hoping you'd take on some ducklings. I'm a teacher at the primary school and I bought some eggs in an incubator so the children could watch them hatch. But now they've hatched and grown bigger they're too lively to keep at school and we don't have a pond for them.'

'Where are they?' I asked her.

'I put the box they're in over by your pond. The ducklings haven't been in water yet – other than their water dish in the incubator tank, which they're always tipping over and sitting and splashing about in.'

We'd almost reached the box when I saw one of the flaps lift and a duckling poke its head out. The next moment the box tipped over and as we started to run towards it six ducklings scrambled out and raced, chirping with excitement, towards the pond.

By the time we got there the little ducklings were swimming about and looking quite at home.

'Will you take them in?' the lady asked, biting her bottom lip. 'I could pay for their upkeep or we could raise some money for them . . . The children would love to come and visit . . .'

'Maybe your school could sponsor the ducklings?' I said, and she thought that was a great idea.

In the distance, I saw the minibus from the old people's home bumping its way along the potholed lane and I headed back to the house to fetch Aurora and Dolores so the old folks could meet them. The minibus was followed by a police car.

'There's been a complaint about one of your dogs, a Great Dane,' the burly policeman said, getting out of the car. He was really looking for Aunt Helen but he found me and Izzy instead. 'Apparently it attacked innocent bystanders at the Highland Games parade.'

Izzy and I started to laugh and the policeman looked cross. 'I can assure you this is no laughing matter.'

I pulled out my phone. 'He was only licking him,' I said, and I showed the policeman the footage of Cyrus trying to take Izzy's collection bucket and then Blue licking him. Now the policeman was laughing too.

'A nice bit of filming,' he said. 'Might come in useful if those three start getting up to tricks again. We've been keeping an eye on them for a while now. Would you be able to email it to the police station? It's Constable Campbell. I was here the other night over the vandalism you had here. There's a few of us who'd like to have a copy of that video.'

I typed in Constable Campbell's email address and then I pressed send. 'Done.'

Blue came over to the policeman and flopped down at his feet. 'You,' Constable Campbell told him, 'might make a very good police dog.'

'I don't think so,' Izzy said. 'He's too soft. Blue would never be able to tackle a real criminal.'

'I wasn't thinking of him for that sort of police work,' Constable Campbell said. 'I was thinking of him for my community police work. When we go into schools and places and talk to folks.'

'Blue'd be good at that,' I said.

'He loves attention and fussing,' said Izzy.

'Let me see what they say at the station, but I think we might be on to a winner,' Constable Campbell told us. 'I've always seen myself with a big dog. And he's a really good big dog, aren't you, boy?'

Blue looked up at him and put out one of his giant paws to shake hands as if he were agreeing.

'Oh no,' I said, when I saw Homer heading towards me. Not that I minded the dog being at the Paw House, not at all. He could come and go as he liked. But I was dreading another meeting with the bullies and everyone knew Homer was Cyrus's dog. I hoped he and his friends weren't here too.

Homer padded over to me and I saw that he'd lost his bandage. I'd have to ask Aunt Helen to put another one on his paw. I didn't want it to get infected. Luckily he wasn't limping any more so it probably wasn't too sore.

The dog wagged his tail and I could see he had something round and yellow in his mouth.

'What have you got, Homer? Is it a toy?' I asked him. It looked like a small Frisbee.

Homer dropped it at my feet and then looked up at me. Definitely not a Frisbee.

'What's this then?' Constable Campbell said, picking it up.

'Please give generously to Lochmarron's First Highland Games,' I read over his shoulder. Homer had been playing with a collection bucket lid. He must have taken it from wherever the thieves were holding their loot!

'This is evidence,' Constable Campbell said as he carefully put the lid inside a plastic bag. 'Good dog, Homer. Good dog!'

Homer looked from one to the other of us and I could tell he liked all the praise.

Rusty was overjoyed to see her friend and ran over to Homer squeeing with delight.

'And now for the waggiest-tail contest,' Aunt Helen's voice said over the microphone.

'Come on you two,' Izzy said to Rusty and Homer and they headed over to the paddock to take part.

'Good luck!' I called after them. I didn't know who would win and it didn't matter. All the animals that lived at the Paw House were winners.

I grabbed some cake from the kitchen and crumbled it up as I ran upstairs to my room.

'Ready, girls?' I said, holding out the crumbs to Dolores and Aurora.

The chickens gobbled up the cake and made happy chicken sounds.

I don't know if it was because I was the one who'd rescued them, or if I had a special affinity with chickens, or that Dolores and Aurora liked the smell of my hair gel. But I ended up walking over to the folks from the old people's home, who were having a cup of tea and some cake in the sunshine, carrying Aurora in my arms and Dolores on top of my head in her little tabard jumper.

The old people, and especially Kenny's mum, Matilda, were entranced by the two chickens in their woollen outfits.

'Don't they look smart?' she said. 'All cosy and warm.'

'Do any of your other animals need knitting for?' an old man asked me.

I thought about the pictures of tortoises wearing knitted shell coats I'd seen on YouTube. But I didn't tell the old people about it because I didn't think Tommy would like wearing one.

'The Paw House could always do with some more knitted blankets and scarves,' I said.

'We'll get right on it!' Matilda told me.

Kenny and Darcy were sitting on the ground next to Matilda. Darcy had her head resting on Kenny's lap.

'Fine day for the open day,' Kenny said.

'You're right about that,' I told him. The weather was glorious.

'Can I hold her?' Matilda asked me, and the next moment Dolores was off my head and sitting happily on Matilda's lap. Matilda gave her a stroke and a little bit of scone every now and again.

Aurora was stroked by just about every one of the old folks and seemed to be in her element as she stretched up her neck and made little clucky sounds.

'Can we adopt them?' one of the old people asked, and Matilda nodded. Everyone seemed to want to.

'They're very easy to look after, and as you can see love being stroked,' I said.

'I think they belong here, actually,' the manager said gently. 'But we could visit them!'

'Every week?' Matilda asked him. 'Make it a regular thing?'

'That's a great idea,' Tania said, coming over with more cakes. 'You could even have lunch and tea and cakes at our new cafe that's going to be open here one day a week.'

The old people all thought that was a very good idea.

'You're sure you'd rather come here than look round the shops like we usually do?' the manager asked them.

'Absolutely!' came the reply from everyone, as Aurora and Dolores pecked up the last of the cake crumbs.

Chapter 20

The open day exceeded all of our expectations. Far more people than we'd hoped for. Just about all the food sold. Tons of people volunteered to help with the animals and made donations – even the American man had made a generous one in honour of his clan. Thank goodness for those old Scottish ancestors! A reporter and photographer from the local paper had turned up and then a crew from Scottish TV had come and filmed Rusty doing her jigsaw puzzle.

Most of the visitors had left by the time we headed over to Mrs Enders' orchard where a caramel-coloured five-month-old alpaca called Toffee that Aunt Helen had offered to foster for a few weeks had been placed temporarily before she was moved to the paddock with Shadow and Gertie.

We'd only just got there when a truck drove up and a man rolled down the window and said, 'Old woman said you took sheep. Got seven weaned lambs in the back.'

'What are you waiting for?' Mrs Enders said, as we all heard the lambs bleating from inside the truck. 'Let the poor things out.'

The man reversed the truck so the rear end of it was facing the orchard, and then unbolted the door.

At first the lambs didn't come out. 'Come on, now!' the man said, hitting the side of the truck with a stick.

'Please don't frighten them,' Aunt Helen said.

But one of the lambs had already half run and half fallen down the truck's metal ramp. It blinked in the bright sunlight. Then it sniffed at the air and looked back at the other lambs. Toffee came over and bent her head down to take a closer look.

The other lambs followed the first one out into the sunshine and the sweet-smelling apple and pear trees of the orchard.

'Right, I'll be going,' the bearded man said. He held out his hand to Mrs Enders. 'This'll help for their upkeep,' he said, giving her a handful of ten-pound notes. 'I'm giving up sheep farming and taking up fruit farming instead. A lot less manure!'

Then he got back in his truck and drove away while we all stared after him.

'Guess I've got lambs in the orchard now!' Mrs Enders chuckled with delight as Aunt Helen and I took Toffee to meet Gertie and Shadow. The old donkey and foal were very interested in the new arrival and soon Shadow and Toffee were running around the paddock together as first she chased Shadow and then he chased her.

Gertie came over to us and I stroked her mane as we watched the two young animals playing.

When Aunt Helen and I got back to the house, I spotted a shiny Jaguar in the yard.

'Hamish! Hamish!' a voice shouted.

I'd got so used to being called Mishka that I almost didn't stop. But when I did my mouth dropped open. What on earth were my mum and dad doing here?

'We ended our trip early to take you home,' Dad said, running towards me.

'But . . .'

'You seemed so short on the phone when we spoke. I'm sorry – you must have missed us so much!' said Mum. She scooped me up in a hug.

'I was filming . . .'

'We changed our flight to Inverness and hired a car so we could come and collect you!' Dad said.

The weather had been perfect for the open day and the new lambs' arrival but now it was starting to spit with rain.

'Time to come home, son,' said Dad.

But I didn't want to go home.

'Come on in,' I said, as the rain grew heavier and I led them into the Paw House and to the dogs' room. Violet and Cullie, Blue, Darcy, Nicole and Mackenzie were there. Cullie ran over to say hello but Dad started sneezing straight away and waving his hands about. Poor Cullie ran straight back to Violet. I could see Mum was very worried about getting any fur on her clothes.

Mackenzie trotted over to her on his three legs, looked up at her with his head to one side and wagged his tail.

'Sweet,' Mum said, although she didn't sound too sure.

Mackenzie sat down and held his paw out to her.

'What's it doing?' Mum asked.

'*His* name's Mackenzie and he wants to shake hands,' I told her.

Mum raised an eyebrow as if she wasn't sure if I was joking or not.

'How do you do,' she said doubtfully to the dog.

Mackenzie rolled on to his back to show off his belly.

'Oh, Helen. Remember how badly we used to want a dog when we were girls?' Mum said to Aunt Helen and I watched in astonishment as she leant over to give Mackenzie's tummy a rub. 'But Mum wouldn't let us? Even made us cross the road if she saw one.'

'You know, now I think about it I think she was really scared of dogs,' Aunt Helen said. 'And that was why she said no.'

'Maybe.'

'What sort of dog is he?' Dad asked Aunt Helen between sneezes as he watched Mum giving Mackenzie a belly rub.

'The lovable kind,' I told him. 'Kisses, Blue!'

Blue immediately got up and lolloped over to me, put his big paws on my shoulders and gave my face a lick.

'Hamish!' Mum cried in horror. 'Germs!'

But I didn't care about that as I gave Blue a stroke.

'He's going to be a community police dog,' I told them.

'He'll make a good one,' Aunt Helen said. 'Won't you, Blue?'

Blue headed over to her and lay down at her feet.

I told Mum and Dad how Blue had chased after Izzy's wellington boot at the Games yesterday.

'Did you know they have Highland Games in Japan too?' Mum asked me.

I shook my head and smiled.

'We've got another trip to Japan arranged for Christmas,' Dad said. 'This time you could come if you like?'

Usually I would have liked to have gone with them more than anything. But things had changed.

'No thanks!' I said.

'What?' Mum and Dad said together.

'Look, you'll get more work done if I'm not there and Aunt Helen said I can come back to the Paw House any time. And I'd really, really like to come back here, if it's OK with you?'

Spending Christmas at the Paw House would be perfect.

'Well . . .'

'If you're really sure you want to spend time with these strays . . .'

'You'd be more than welcome to come too,' Aunt Helen told Mum and Dad.

'And,' I said. 'I've decided I want to sponsor the Paw House – with the money Grandad left me.'

'That's not what it was intended for,' Mum said, surprised.

Well, I thought to myself, *I can do what I like once I'm eighteen.*

'I want you to keep your inheritance, Mishka,' Aunt Helen said, sounding upset. 'Not everything's about money. You're one amazing, unstoppable person when you put your mind to something. And you know what? I'd pay *you* to come here and help!'

She gave me a hug and I pushed my face into her baggy-jumper-covered shoulder, which was good because no one could see the stupid tear that ran out of my eye and down my face.

I really didn't want to leave Aunt Helen and the Paw House but I couldn't refuse to go. And I still had school and exams in Edinburgh. But one day I'd come for good and in the meantime I'd come every holiday I could.

I made sure I said goodbye to all the animals before I left. Darcy would be moving in with Kenny soon and I knew she'd be happy with him.

'You have a nice rest of your life,' I told her.

Violet and Cullie would soon be with Irene and Ray, starting a whole new adventure of their own.

'Goodbye, little pup. And I'll miss you, Violet.'

Nicole licked my hand when I stroked her old head. I was glad she'd get to spend her last years here.

'Back in a bit,' I said to Mum and Dad.

'Don't be too long. We've got a five-hour drive home,' Mum said, as Aunt Helen handed Dad some kitchen roll to sneeze into.

Mackenzie came with me when I went to say goodbye to the rest of the animals.

Rusty and Homer were both outside and lying together on the garden lounger Mrs Enders had been sitting on the other day.

'You two look comfortable,' I said, giving them a stroke before Mackenzie and I headed over to the barn.

'Bye, Custard,' I said, kissing her head. 'See you, Peaches.' I gave her a stroke and a carrot. 'I'll be back really soon.'

Woolly and Jock got a slice of bread each and Gertie and Shadow and Toffee an apple. Tommy was over in the barn for once so he got a bit of apple too. I could just spot the mother cat and her kittens hidden in the corner. Safe.

Izzy was in Chicken Castle feeding the chickens. They had a new turkey with them now. Dolores and Aurora were there too, but in their own separate run for the meantime. I gave them both a stroke.

'Watch this,' Izzy said, as she held out her arms and the turkey ran into them for a hug. 'Apparently turkeys love hugs!'

I shook my head. 'Who would have guessed?'

'What's wrong?' she asked.

I told her that I was leaving, at least for a while.

'Just make sure you come back soon,' she said.

'I will. Just make sure you stay out of trouble,' I said.

Izzy grinned. 'Won't be any trouble now Cyrus is being sent back to school,' she told me. 'Steenie texted me to let me know. Constable Campbell found the parade money at Cyrus's house and although the Highland Games committee aren't pressing charges his dad's decided it'd be best if Cyrus goes back to boarding school early. Donut and Jay are a couple of sooks when he's not around.'

I turned round as Rusty and Homer came in behind me.

'Oh, and it looks like Homer's staying here for good now,' Izzy said, as the dog looked up at me. 'Cyrus's dad said he couldn't manage him!'

'Good,' I said, and I bent down to give Homer a stroke and Rusty a scratch. 'I'm going to miss you, though, little piglet.'

'Not if you turn on your television!' Izzy said. 'STV want to do a whole programme about her and the rest of the animals at the sanctuary.'

So Rusty was going to become the star she deserved to be. I thought about Omar's cat and smiled. My YouTube dream had become a reality after all – I just never expected it to be with a pig!

I headed back to Mum and Dad.

'Bye, Mishka,' said Aunt Helen, as she hugged me goodbye. 'Having you here has changed so many things.'

'Well, being here has changed *everything* for me,' I told her, hugging her back.

'I'll miss you,' she said.

'Not for long,' I told her. 'I'll be coming back the next chance I get.' And texting every day to check how she and all the animals were doing in the meantime.

I craned my neck to look out of the back window of the car as we drove off – past an SPCA van that was driving in with another animal needing Aunt Helen's help.

'I'll be back!' I called out of my window. 'Soon – I promise!'

Aunt Helen waved and waved, as an SPCA officer led a very thin spaniel over to her. As Aunt Helen knelt down to meet her newest Paw House guest, Mackenzie looked at me, tilted his head to one side, gave a quick bark, and lifted his paw as if to say goodbye.

Acknowledgements

The idea for this story began one snowy Christmas when Traffy, Bella, Eric and I stayed in a cottage in Wester Ross close to the Applecross Peninsula. The wintry scenery was stunning and the wildlife very exciting to spot. We made friends with fellow dog-loving locals and their dogs – which I've done wherever I happen to be with a dog in the world – dogs just seem to bring people together!

When I was a child my grandmother and grandfather owned a smallholding in Buckinghamshire and often had rescued animals there, including a cat named Juno and two dogs called Patch and Petra. Petra had been a stray for many years before she came to them and was a seasoned escape artist. Once she was gone for days, although usually it was only a few hours, before she turned up again. I remember there was a pony no one wanted and two elderly sheep. There were geese that were very protective of their field and would honk and squawk to tell intruders to go away – unless you had something tasty for them to eat. There were rabbits and chickens too, but although as children we loved meeting and holding the chicks we didn't spent much time with the chickens, other than feeding them, and so we never realized how intelligent and loving they can be. When my dear grandmother passed away and my grandfather grew older there were fewer and fewer animals, but there was still the tame robin he used to feed that came to sit on his shovel when he was working in the garden. When he was very old my grandfather had a canary, which came to live with me after he passed away. I couldn't bear for the canary to be kept in a locked cage and so the door was always left open and he went in and out as he pleased.

The Paw House story is very close to my heart and I'm so delighted that Penguin Random House are publishing it. The research has been fascinating, often heart-warming but sometimes heart-breaking. I met lots of people and spoke to different charities trying to improve the lot of all sorts of animals. I also met those who are trying to improve the lot of people by matching them with animals.

Huge thanks must go to my editor Emma Jones who has been so enthusiastic about this book throughout. Copy editor Jennie Roman and Stephanie Barrett, and proofreader Beatrix McIntyre. The wonderful cover design by Dominica Clements and final illustration by Angelo Rinaldi. On the PR and sales front many thanks must go to Ellen Grady and Beth O'Brien as well as Nicola O'Connell for foreign rights. Last but definitely not least my agent and friend Clare Pearson who's been a part of this book since I first thought of writing it, years ago. Writing with a great professional team around you makes all the difference! As does a supportive home front.

When Freya came to live with us she became the inspiration for Cullie. Our older dog Bella – although not as delighted at the sight of Freya as Violet was at meeting Cullie – helped to inspire Violet's role. Bella and Freya are the perfect writing companions and as soon as I sit down at the computer they know it's time for them to have a snooze – but when I stand up Bella's usually got her ball lying next to her, all ready for a play.

My husband Eric has always been and continues to be a valued listener, advice giver, research helper and best friend. He's taken Bella and Freya to the lake, where they love to swim, while I finish writing this. Once it's done I will be joining them.

Recipes

There are many ways in which we can all help animals. Even the smallest of actions can make a big difference. Lots of birds enjoy pecking at apples, pears and other soft fruit, as well as carrots. You could even make a tasty treat for a hungry mouth or beak.

Bird Food Balls

Garden birds love having a saucer of water put out for them along with some bird food. The recipe below is very easy and fun to make.

You will need:

- 50g coconut oil
- 2 tablespoons of peanut butter
- 20g flour
- 100g oats
- Bag of wild birdseed

How to make them:

Combine all of the ingredients in a large bowl and mix together. Shape into balls or simply put the mixture in your bird feeder (which is what I did). My dogs thought this food looked delicious and licked out the bowl. So I made them some banana ice cream instead – and then added some peanut butter to it because they LOVE peanut butter (but check it doesn't have xylitol as this is bad for dogs).

Banana Ice Cream – ***for animals and people***

Slice up a banana or two and put them in the freezer. After a couple of hours take the bananas out, whizz them up in the blender (or let them defrost a little and mash up with a fork or the potato masher) and they turn into soft yummy ice cream – and then you can add your favourite topping – we like peanut butter!

Don't forget the hedgehogs!

They love to eat cat or dog food (not fish-based) left out for them in the garden. But I can't do this because my dogs would gobble it all up!

Turn the page for an extract from

Echo Come Home

by Megan Rix

AVAILABLE NOW

www.meganrix.com

Chapter 1

Jake watched the shaggy-coated little dog through the supermarket window as he waited for his mum and younger sister, Vicky, to fetch a trolley. The dog wagged its tail every time someone dropped a coin into the homeless man's cap. Jake smiled. It was almost like the little dog was saying thank you.

'Excuse me,' a voice behind Jake said, but Jake didn't move. 'Excuse me!' the voice repeated more loudly. Finally, the man shook his head and pushed his trolley round the boy.

Eleven-year-old Jake didn't realize that he was standing in people's way by the door and he was oblivious to the black looks he was getting from shoppers trying to get past him with their trolleys.

He wished he had a dog. A dog that would spend all day with him and always be there for him, like the homeless man's dog was.

'Excuse me . . . you're in my way . . . Can you just move . . . for goodness' sake!'

Jake turned in surprise as a trolley bumped into the back of him. He stared at the shopper's angry face. Her lips opened and closed as she spoke.

'. . . rude boy . . .' he lip-read, before the woman bustled on into the supermarket.

Jake flinched and his face burned red as he turned back to look at the dog. Now it was sitting on the pavement next to the old homeless man. It held its paw out to Jake's mum and eight-year-old Vicky.

‘Spare a few coins, lady?’ said the homeless man.

The little grizzle-coated terrier cross stood up and wagged his tail. His head tilted to one side as he looked up at them. Jake watched his mum drop some coins into the man’s cap.

‘Thank you kindly,’ Jake lip-read.

‘Jake!’ Vicky yelled, when she saw her brother through the glass.

‘Shh, Vicky,’ her mum said. ‘You know he can’t hear you.’

‘Why didn’t he wait for us to get the trolley? He’s always wandering off and then we have to chase after him,’ Vicky grumbled. ‘He can be a right pain sometimes.’

Once they’d gone, the homeless man took the coins out of his cap and put them in his pocket. He grinned at the little dog. ‘You bring old George luck, you do, Bones,’ he said.

The little dog’s tail wagged.

'Afternoon, George,' a young man in a brown suit said, coming over to them. 'Lovely day.'

'Can't complain,' George said, as he tugged at the tattered red-and-white spotted bandana he liked to wear round his neck. It was very warm for March.

'How've you been keeping?'

'Not too bad, Mr C. Can't complain.'

He knew Charles Cooper from way back. The first time they'd met, Mr C, as everyone called him, had been a student running the food bank. George hadn't seen him for a while though, not since he'd dished up the roast potatoes at the Christmas lunch for the homeless they had every year at the town hall. George still thought about those potatoes. He'd even dreamt about them once.

'Heard you'd been promoted,' George said.

Mr Cooper nodded. 'I'm going to be running the Fresh Start Hostel over by the park. You should come and see how the building work's progressing, George. The place is going to be fit for a king once it's done.'

But George wasn't even sure he wanted to live at the hostel yet. He didn't like the thought of all those walls closing in around him. Or of the doors trapping him in at night. He wanted to be free to come and go as he pleased, especially when the weather was warm like today. Although in the winter, when the nights grew bitter and his bones ached from the cold, maybe a hostel wouldn't be such a bad place to live. It'd be warm and Mr C would make sure there was always plenty to eat. Maybe even dish up some of those roast potatoes.

'That your dog, George?' Mr Cooper asked him.

George shook his head. 'He's not anyone's dog but his own. I call him Bones because I get him one from the butcher's when I can. Bones loves his bones.'

Mr Cooper reached over to stroke the dog, but Bones backed away.

'Doesn't like to be stroked,' George said, as the young man tried to coax the dog to him. 'At least not until he gets to know you, and sometimes not even then.'

'Why not?' Mr Cooper asked. But George didn't know the answer to that.

From a safe distance the little dog looked up at him with his big brown eyes and wagged his tail.

'Having him around reminds me of what it used to be like,' George said softly, almost to himself.

'What used to be like?'

'Having a home and someone who cares about you.'

'You could have that again once the new hostel opens in the summer. All it takes is that first step. There's going to be a festival in the park to celebrate its opening and raise funds to keep it running. I'm on my way to help design the posters for it now.'

George's watery, tired blue eyes looked up at Mr Cooper. He'd had enough of hearing about the hostel.

'Spare a bit of change, guv? For the dog,' he said.

Mr Cooper sighed and dropped some coins into George's cap.

Bones came back to George once Mr C had gone.

'I wish I could give you a proper home,' the old man said. 'You deserve somewhere warm and safe with lots of good food.' He didn't know if the Fresh Start Hostel would allow pets or not, but most places didn't.

The little dog whined and put out his paw.

'Well, at least we'll both have something nice to eat today and some for the others, too,' George said. He groaned as he stood up and headed off down the street with Bones trotting along beside him.

First they went to the butcher's to get a bone and then they visited the fish and chip shop.

'As many chips as this'll buy,' George said, as he emptied his pockets of all the coins they'd collected.

Mandy looked over at the little dog waiting for George outside the door. It reminded her of the dog she'd had when she was a little girl. As a special treat, she gave George far more chips than his money would normally have bought.

'There you go,' she said. 'I put a bit of leftover fish in there too. And this is for your dog.' She held out a saveloy.

'Thank you.'

George took the saveloy from her, scooped up the hot bags of chips and fish from the counter and headed out of the shop.

Mandy watched through the window as the little dog wolfed down the saveloy in a few big gulps. George gave her a thumbs up and she waved back.

'Come on, Bones,' George said.

He didn't hear the swish of the skateboard's wheels as it headed along the pavement, but Bones did and he gave a bark. George looked round just in time and was able to step back before the skateboard and its rider ran into him.

'Thank you,' George said to Bones. It wasn't the first time the little dog had alerted him to something that he hadn't heard coming.

The two of them walked down to the river on the outskirts of town. Under the bridge other homeless people gathered at night for shelter and company.

The chips weren't hot by the time George and Bones arrived, but they weren't cold either, and everyone was grateful as George handed round the delicious salty fried potatoes and leftover fish.

'There you go, Mike . . . This is for you, Jen . . . Here you are, Harvey . . . Cole, Blue . . . Jay, Kel . . .'

The little dog lay down on the muddy ground beneath the bridge and started gnawing on his bone.

'Always get more money when he's with me,' George said, as the rest of them ate.

'Got more in one day than I usually get in a week when he spent the day with me,' Jen agreed.

'Missed him when he took himself off,' said Harvey, as he ate his chips with one hand and sketched the dog on the paper the chips had been wrapped in with the other. Bones had been gone for weeks and none of them knew where he'd disappeared to, just like they didn't know where he'd come from when he first turned up. A little dog without a collar and a fear of being stroked, at least until he got to know you, and sometimes not even then.

They were all glad when he'd come back home to the bridge and not just because of the increase in the money they could collect. Everyone felt happier when Bones was around, but they knew he could take off at any moment. He didn't belong to anyone.

'Never known a dog to dislike being stroked before,' Mike said.

'Something bad must have happened,' said George, and the others nodded.

As it grew darker, the people who lived under the bridge settled down for the night. For the moment it served as a windbreak and an umbrella from the rain, but the bridge was condemned and none of them knew how long it would be before it was taken down meaning they would lose the only home they had.

*

Read all the heart-warming animal stories by Megan Rix . . .

'If you love Michael Morpurgo, you'll enjoy this'
Sunday Express

AVAILABLE NOW

www.meganrix.com